RAFE

Out of a Union prisoner-of-war camp, Rafe had worked his way West and found his family again, all of them working one of the best horse ranches in the Arizona territory. But he soon found out there was a rotten deal afoot to swindle his folks out of their home—and that the ramrod, Spangler, was in it up to his hatbrim. Spangler was a tough man to come up against. Rafe found that out the hard way after being ambushed, beaten-up and left to die. But the tide was turned the day Rafe got his split-second's edge.

RAFE

Nelson Nye

CURLEY LARGE PRINT
HAMPTON, NEW HAMPSHIRE

Library of Congress Cataloging-in-Publication Data

Nye, Nelson C. (Nelson Coral), 1907–
    Rafe / Nelson C. Nye.
      p. cm.
    ISBN 0-7927-1775-9 (hardcover).
    ISBN 0-7927-1774-0 (softcover)
    1. Large type books. I. Title.
[PS3527.Y33R28   1993]   93-25405
813'.54—dc20   CIP

British Library Cataloguing in Publication Data available

This Large Print edition is published by Chivers Press, England, and by Curley Large Print, an imprint of Chivers North America, 1993.

Published by arrangement with Golden West Literary Agency.

U.K. Hardcover ISBN 0 7451 2000 8
U.K. Softcover   ISBN 0 7451 2012 1
U.S. Hardcover ISBN 0 7927 1775 9
U.S. Softcover   ISBN 0 7927 1774 0

Copyright © 1962 by Ace Books. Renewed ® 1990 by Nelson C. Nye.
Copyright © 1993 in the British Commonwealth.
All rights reserved.

All characters in this book are fictitious. Any resemblance to actual persons, living or dead, is purely coincidental.

Printed in Great Britain

CHAPTER ONE

It was hotter than the bottom of Lucifer's skillet. Heat hung like smoke above the Sulfur Springs Valley, turning the Cherrycows gray as slate; and the lesser mountains north and south were almost lost in the shimmering haze that draped them like a tangle of cobwebs.

The hands stood straight up on Rafe's tarnished watch and, squinting into the glare, he cursed. He had run out of grub the other side of the pass and two mornings ago had chewed the last of his jerky; his canvas watersack, snagged by thorns, refused to yield even so much as a gurgle. Pitching it away in disgust he stepped down, for his skewbald mare was about at the end of her rope by the look. Peering into the sky he shook a fist at the buzzards. 'Bastards!' he croaked in a cracked off-key whisper.

He was a yellow-haired man, gaunt in ragged red shirt and baggy-kneed trousers. The yellow silk of a Confederate cavalry sash was partially obscured by a brush scarred vest which had once cost money and was attractively spangled with flowers embroidered by somebody's needle. Likewise showing a deal of hard usage were the boots into which his pants had been stuffed, but the spurs were silver and bright as new coins where the sun struck across them.

Now his eyes sharpened. A streamer of dust crept up out of the west. Coming from low hills were a number of specks; horses, Rafe decided, and humping along like the devil beating tanbark.

Straight out across the flats they spilled in a ragged line, hellity-larrup like a bunch of red Indians. They were still too far off to be heard but would cross his tracks hardly a quarter mile away. He climbed back on the mare and, swinging his reins, whipped her forward in a shambling run.

It was all open here, a cactus-strewn waste of wind-riffled sand. What air there was was like the breath from a furnace, but as the horsebackers bore down he started waving his hat in great circles, hoarsely shouting to make sure he was sighted.

There were seven in the bunch—he could see that much. They showed no intention of pulling up or veering toward him. Badly rattled, Rafe fired his six-shooter. They couldn't fail to hear that.

When they kept straight on he could scarcely believe his own eyes. They never even turned their heads to peer back at him.

He pulled the floundering mare to a halt, conscious of the trembling of her legs beneath the leathers. Some of the things he yelled would have set a white oak post to smoking. But the outfit kept on, a swirling, swift-dwindling column of dust eventually lost against the far horizon.

Long before this Rafe was out of the saddle, dragging the black-and-white mare by the reins, shouting and cursing, plunging furiously after them, stumbling, falling, scrambling crab-fashion up and erratically staggering, the breath sawing through his cracked lips like gagging. Not until exhaustion left him sprawled on the sand like a ruptured duck did he finally give up, great tears of rage rolling over the weather-toughened, beard-stubbled cheeks.

When reason returned and he got his chin from the grit, the yonder slopes were red with the last rays of the sun. He got up slowly, half fried from the heat, his bleared vision taking in the empty waterless flats, the barren hills all about. A terrible sigh welled out of him. The mare lay on her side, spavined legs stuck out, half sunk in the burning sand, tied to his fate by the reins still clutched in a tight shut fist.

It took a good while, a deal of yanking and prodding, to convince the fool critter she was not beyond aid. Moving around to her rear he tailed her like a bogged-down cow. He got her hind end up and there she stuck, groaning piteously. He might have gone off and left her if his case hadn't been so desperate. He whacked her rump with a piece of rope cactus; she lunged onto her feet squealing like a stuck pig. Then she whirled, ears flat, trying to bite when he caught up with her. A lump of sugar from his pockets consummated an uneasy truce. Reins bent over his shoulder he set off, pointing east, in the tracks left by the inhospitable seven.

He lost count of the times their waning strength forced halts. Ever and again they went stumbling on while the moon came up and millions of stars winked down, bright as sparkling emeralds; but Rafe had no mind for beauty. There was a bulldog clamp to the thrust of his jaw and he kept his stare hard-fixed to the trail.

But even a concentration as indomitable as his could not withstand entirely the needs and adjustments of nature. He was seeing things now which no longer had substance—faces and shapes floating out of his past. He was beginning to babble the croakings and gibberish that accompany delirium. His father's face came up out of the tracks. He saw young Duke and his sister Luce, the hardscrabble hills of the Bender farm with the sedge pushing up from the worn out earth, the frowsy tangle of sassafras and locust, just as he remembered from the day he'd gone off with his squirrel rifle to find Jeb Stuart and whip the Yanks.

Eleven years ago! It seemed like only

yesterday he had marched away with a heart filled to bursting and a head full of nonsense. There hadn't been a bit of romance to it! War was blood and guts and the stink of broken bodies. Cannon smoke and bullet screech, the screams and curses of mutilated men.

He was screaming himself as the ugly sights took shape in his brain. The skewbald mare reared back on her bits, snorting and shaking; by main strength he dragged her on into the flare and the flashings while the big guns rumbled and banged all about him. Retching and grasping he went stumbling on through the stinking mud, his one good hand holding hard to the reins, mind clenched fierce to his faith in Jeb Stuart—someway old Beauty would pull him clear.

Next thing he knew he was flat in the mud—sticky and slimy as a fistful of slobbers. The moon was gone and a cold wind blew, whining through the sparse grass and ghostly patches of chaparral; far away on his right tiny points of light were blinking like a huddle of fireflies.

He didn't know, by God, if he could get up or not, but he finally made it. The growth near enough to touch and to feel was beaded with moisture and the night wasn't far enough gone for dew. He had no memory of rain, but the clammy bind of his sodden clothes and the quaggy give of the ground underfoot appeared to imply there'd been patches of time which had got clean away from him.

A peculiar sound, like castanets, crept into his notice and was suddenly pinned down for the chatter of teeth; with this awareness he began shivering and shaking as the damp bit deeper into his bones. He guessed he was probably coming down with something. His head felt funny and his face, when he touched it, was hot as a stove lid. He knew damned well he couldn't walk another mile.

He tried to get onto the skewbald mare but his foot and the stirrup wouldn't get together. He got hold of the horn but his bumbling attempts to heave himself up eventually wore out the animal's patience. With a panicked snort she flung up her head and fled from his reach.

The goddamn wind was rough as a cob. It shoved him around like a cork on a fishline. When the lights spun into his vision again he set off, stumbling toward them, muttering like a man in his cups. He saw Duke again, the Old Man and his mother, the sidehill farm that was back in the Ozarks and the bulltongue plow he had bucked through the stumps.

He was back in the smoke of battle once more, down flat on his face with an arm doubled under the dead weight of his horse and the fires of hell tearing through him like splinters. He heard the hoofs pounding round him, the clashing of sabers; and the next thing he knew he was in a Yank prison. Then the war was over and he was hunting his folks. Someone else had the farm, they'd never heard of the Benders. Elsie Potts, whom he'd rolled in the hay, said his people had took off West in a wagon.

So Rafe had come West. Missouri, Kansas, the Indian nations. He had lost them in Texas. Five years he'd put in trying to pick up the trail, riding for ranchers, buying hides, driving stage. Finally, working out of Brady, he'd hitched on with a freighter. Near El Paso he'd took up last winter with some pretty hardcases holed up in the Van Horns, making a living of sorts stopping coaches. One of them fellers had come from Colorado.

Was some Benders, he had said, in the horse raising business somewheres west of Shakespeare, over in Arizona Territory. He didn't know much about them except their iron was on some pretty fast steppers. Had been mounted on one himself, he claimed, till a Wells Fargo messenger with a sawed-off Greener had blasted this gelding plumb out from under him. Best damn bronc a man ever straddled.

Along about there someplace Rafe's fever broke and he fell into a sound sleep.

Next time he got his eyes open to know

about it, the first things he glimpsed were the peeled yesocoated poles of a sod roof. That took some studying. Presently his glance, dropping down a whitewashed wall, stopped at a window through which sunlight was pouring in a golden flood. Through scrinched up lids he stared incredulously at a set of lace curtains, wondering what fool was so out of his mind as to hang such geegaws against dirt walls.

The skreak of a chair, the long bend of a shadow, drew his eyes to the side. There was a halo of hair not two foot away from him. Then her features took shape, appearing to float over him—which was when Rafe knew that by some flip he had got off the track and bumbled into heaven.

He got up on one elbow the better to see. He was pretty near carried away, sure enough. Lips red as cherries. China doll eyes and dimples—Lord! Handsome, he thought, as an ace-full on kings, so sweet bee trees was gall beside her. Never knowing he'd been tucked into a bed he sat straight up and found her hand against him. Her eyes got big. Rafe suddenly discovered he was naked as a rock.

★   ★   ★

When he finally came out from under the covers, still flushed of face and plenty mortified besides, the girl was gone. In her place sat a man who looked bigger than a load of hay with the poles up. He sure had tallow. Three sets of chins, and most of the rest of him looked to Rafe like stomach. You'd of had to throw a diamond hitch to keep him in a saddle.

It was hard to know what to make of so much bulk, and while Rafe was trying the three chins twisted round, the great head tipping back in an attitude of listening while the eyes, nearly buried in the arroyos and billows of a network of wrinkles behind that great reddish lump of a nose, sneaked a stealthy look in the direction of a door that was not quite closed.

Apparently reassured, the head came forward with a kind of grunt, a hand shot out, dipping from sight beneath the bed to be presently resurrected wrapped about an unmarked bottle of what appeared to be rye whisky. The other hand wrestled the cork from its neck. But just as he straightened, making ready to lift it, a light tapping of heels just beyond the door turned him stiff as a poker.

His eyes took in Rafe and became flat as fish scales. The three chins quivered, the vast bulk jiggled, appearing to heave as with inner convulsions, and somewhere in the process the bottle disappeared.

The door was pushed open. The girl

again. Slim as a willow shoot and, even in the made-over dress she had on, a vision so lovely it made Rafe blink. 'Oh—' she cried, stopping, 'you've waked up! How do you feel?'

With his tongue clapped against the roof of his mouth Rafe couldn't do more than gulp and goggle. Never had he got his sights on anyone able to upset him the way she was. He had the same nerve-shattering blinding impulse to get up and run that stampedes cattle—the flap of a blanket would have set him off. And yet, incredibly, he liked looking at her. The put-up hair was like burnished kettle copper and her eyes in this light looked the shade of blue larkspur all sparkling and misty with morning dew.

She came over and fluffed up his pillow. 'Are you hungry?' she asked, considering him, smiling.

The bulk in the chair heaved and puffed like a porpoise, clearing its throat like a rattle of stones coming down a tin chute. 'Goddlemighty, girl—been three days, ain't it? Go fix the boy something before he expires!'

Picking up her skirts, prettily flushing, the girl turned and fled.

A clanking of stove lids came almost at once, a banging of pots interspersed other sounds. The bottle reappeared and the red-nosed old walrus with the milkweed hair took a couple hearty swigs, smacking his lips as he drove home the cork before resetting it under Rafe's covers. He raised a finger in front of his mouth, rheumy eyes twinkling amiably. 'Mum's the word, eh, laddie?'

Then the old duffer sighed. 'All right, boy. Get it off your chest afore you burst.'

'Three days I've been here! Where am I?' Rafe growled.

'You ain't looking at St. Pete, that's for sure. This here's the town of Dry Bottom. About three steps from hell.'

This didn't mean a heap to Rafe, but the way those eyes in that tub of lard kept flattening and swelling was enough to set a man's teeth on edge. The whole deal was unsettling, three days gone straight out of your life, waking up with no clothes in someone else's bed, and then this feller. Rafe would about as soon have been watched by a cobra.

'That—girl?' he gruffed, swallowing, nervous.

'Matter of opinion. My keeper, some would tell you, and they wouldn't be far wrong.' The vast bulk heaved as with internal convulsions. If Rafe hadn't known better he might of figured the old fool was growed to that chair; he sure didn't look like he could get around much with his short stumpy arms and great barrels for legs. He was the craziest sight Rafe had ever run into, and yet—those damned eyes, the way they swelled up and flattened, always picking and prying, seemed to dig right into a man's quivering marrow.

Rafe snorted to think he could be such a ninny. 'Well,' he said, defiant, 'who is she?'

'Name's Bunny. You may be hard put to believe this, but she happens to be my daughter.' He cleared his throat with an avalanche of sound so sharp and sudden Rafe's good hand shot out to clamp hold of the bed. 'I'm Wilbur Pike,' the old walrus said, seeming to own to it grudgingly, afterwards growling, 'Who're you?'

'Yell "Rafe" and I'll come if I'm in shoutin' distance.'

'That all the handle you got?' Pike said.

There was a limit to how beholden a man ought to be, and Rafe didn't figure it included personal history especially since he hadn't asked to be saved, and particular by no he-hog who was living off a chit of a girl and sneaking drinks every time she turned her back. He shut his eyes, feeling kind of lightheaded, but they came open quick enough when the old boozer said, 'Somebody camped on your shirt tail, boy?'

'Look,' Rafe snarled, 'if you don't want me here just fetch my clothes an' I'll shake your dust so golram fast—'

'Tsk, tsk, tsk. If there's nobody hunting you, why so edgy? You're being took care of.'

Pike leaned forward, grunting a little, and it was like a damp wind coming off a distillery. 'You want a shot at that elixir?'

So tangled and excited he was pretty near shaking, Rafe threw back the covers and sat up. He was trying to find the floor with his feet when he heard the girl coming. With a burn blazing through the anemic look of his cheeks he was forced to get back and yank the sheets up again.

Bunny appeared with a bowl and some crackers. She could see he was riled, and looked at her father. The old reprobate grinned. 'He was fixing to get up and put on his duds.'

'Oh, he mustn't,' Bunny cried, hurrying over, blue eyes reproachful. 'Why, you're weak as a kitten.' She put a hand on his forehead. 'He's burning up!'

'It's the exposure,' Pike wheezed. 'He'll feel better when some of that broth gets into him.'

She set the bowl and the crackers on a stool and bent to lift and prop the pillows back of him. She got an arm under his shoulders. 'Scrooch up a little. There ... that's more like it.'

The clean woman smell of her was like an ambrosia, albeit somewhat disconcerting with so much of her so close. Rafe, self-conscious as a cow in bloomers, ungraciously growled, 'I can feed myself!'

'Well ...' she said, stepping back, 'go ahead.' She handed him the bowl and the crackers and a spoon, still hovering over him, blue eyes dark with concern. The old tub, watching, chuckled silent as an Indian. Then his look winnowed down. 'What's the matter with that hand?'

Seemed for a moment Rafe wasn't going to answer. He couldn't conceal his awkwardness and apparently his pride was touchy about it. Then his glance, crossing Bunny's, kind of yawned away. 'Arm wasn't set right. Horse rolled on it.'

Bunny's eyes got awfully big. 'In the war?' she whispered.

Rafe testily nodded. He managed to get the bowl anchored with the paw, transferring the spoon to his good left hand. 'Didn't waste much pains on us Rebels up north.'

'Daddy could fix it.'

Rafe nearly missed his mouth with the spoon. Way he looked at Pike he would sooner have sawed the arm off. 'Reckon I can live with it.'

'If he's pig-headed enough, I guess,' Bunny said, 'a man can live with anything.'

When Rafe didn't back off enough to open his mouth, her chin came up. 'Dad was the best man on bones in Grant's army!'

Rafe crumbled the crackers into his broth. With his eyes on the bowl he began spooning it into him.

14

Bunny glared resentfully. Her father cleared his throat. 'How long did they keep you out of circulation?'

'Till the end of the war—two years,' Rafe said, his tone making it plain he'd had enough on that subject.

When the bowl was empty Rafe held it out. 'That wasn't half bad,' he gruffed, 'for a sample. If you got any more, how about throwin' in a couple dozen dog bones?'

It began to appear that Bunny might have a bit of temperature herself. Never in all her born days, she was thinking indignantly, had she come up against a more uncivilized specimen. If this hadn't been one of her most cherished bowls—the only one left of Great Aunt Delia's orange blossom set—she'd have been mightily tempted to wham it right down on his shaggy-haired head.

She shot a glance at her father.

'Why not?' Pike shrugged. 'Wasn't that mutt of Pearly Smith's digging a while ago in that bed where you set out those rose cuttings? If two years in a Yankee prison wasn't able to put this joker out of business, a dirty old bone isn't likely to bother him. Go ahead and get it.'

It was a pity to find all this irony wasted. But what could you expect of an unreconstructed Rebel? You could go on and talk till you were blue in the face but there wasn't any law that impelled them to listen. That exasperating man had his mouth open, snoring!

CHAPTER TWO

No sooner had they gone than Rafe, turned quiet, cautiously opened one eye. By the bend and color of the sun coming in it was apparent the evening was pretty well along. He looked around for his clothes. 'A pretty kettle of fish!' he growled when, unable to discover them, he shoved his legs out from under the bedding. Whatever this pair had in their minds for him it boded no good, he was convinced of that.

In the light of past experience he could hardly be blamed for his dark suspicions. Over in West Texas a law-abiding Rebel didn't have no more rights than chicken has drawers. Carpetbaggers was all over that country, grabbing and yanking like a clutch of snapping turtles, confiscating ranches and every sort of business that might be bludgeoned into yielding faintest sign of a profit. What couldn't be snatched by sheer push and beller they picked up through the courts at twenty cents on the dollar. Any Godfearing native that cared to keep up his health had to learn to eat crow and bow and scrape like a lackey while they took away his substance and made tramps of his women. Rafe was almighty sure this redhaired Delilah and her overgrown moose of a father hadn't done what they was doing out of plain Christian charity or the milk of human kindness. There was a long sharp hook tucked away in this deal some place.

He had felt a sight better in that bed than he did on his feet. With the sweat cracking through the pores of his skin he shook like a shaft of wheat in a windstorm, swaying and jiggling bad as Pike's three chins. The room dived and rocked like a cork in a millrace while the broth sloshed inside him till he expected any moment to find it spewed on the floor.

He took hold of the bed with both hands, locking his teeth until the room settled down. He hadn't come nearer groaning in the war with that horse on him. He couldn't figure how he come to be so danged poorly, so paperbacked and gut-shrunk, without that pair had poisoned him.

Holding fast to whatever was handiest he finally got as far from the bed as the chest with the tin-framed Mexican mirror hung over it. Maybe they'd stashed his clothes in here. At least he might come across a weapon, something to give him hope of getting clear.

The first drawer he looked in was empty except for a sachet of scent and a flutter of bright colored frilly squares hardly bigger than gunpatches that it finally got through to him must be some kind of dandified nose blowers. The next drawer stuck. When it finally came loose he jumped back white as chalk.

It was no snake made his eyes bug out like knots or the breath so rattly sounding in his throat. With cheeks red as fire he slammed the drawer shut, remembering the curtains, wildly staring at the bed, seeing now the God Bless sampler, the embroidery on the pillows; knowing at last, aghast, the girl had given up her room, indeed her very own bed to him!

Catching a glimpse of his face in the hand-rolled wavery glass of the mirror he staggered, clammy, on legs that seemed no firmer than rubber till, finding the bed against the backs of his knees, he collapsed with a quaver.

Never had he felt more mortification or been prey to such a host of conflicting emotions till it abruptly came over him that these people were Yankees. He got the sheet up, covering his nakedness and, thus reminded of it, felt a little better; even then he couldn't get halfways comfortable. Putting him here was just a part of the trap—they sure as hell figured to get *something* out of him.

With this salubrious thought his punished

flesh overcame him and he slipped down a dark spiral into the black of exhausted sleep.

★   ★   ★

He felt more nearly himself the next time he roused and found her hand on his forehead. It looked to be mid-morning, the room filled with sunshine and delectable odors which he shortly discovered to be emanating from the tray reposing on a nearby stool.

Bunny, cheerfully smiling, voiced a friendly good morning, helped him sit up, bunched the pillows behind him. Then she fetched up the tray which she laid across his lap, whisked off the cloth and advised him to pitch in.

Rafe didn't wait for additional urging. He was hungry enough to bite a bear with the hide on.

Bacon and eggs, a great heaping plate of them. Coffee in a pot. Toast with real butter, and strawberry preserves. 'If there's anything else you want, just holler.'

He contained himself till the door shut behind her, then he grabbed up the fork. The bacon and most of the eggs went down like a jugful of syrup being poured through a sieve. And the first cup of java. The third piece of toast took a little longer; when he got it inside him he was filled to the gills. He did eventually swallow a little more of the coffee. He was glad to lean back and let her pick up the tray.

This time she was gone for maybe half an hour. Rafe fetching her back with howls for his clothes. What she brought was a washcloth and razor and a mug with a brush in it.

Rafe said suspiciously, 'What's them for?'

'Don't you want to freshen up?'

'What I want is my clothes!'

'Patience,' she smiled. 'Mending a body isn't done in one day.'

'If you think,' Rafe glared, 'I'm about to be a guinea pig for your ol' man—'

'Don't you want to get your strength back?'

'I'll git it back, don't you worry about that!'

She considered him doubtfully. 'Well, I'll speak to Daddy.'

'What is this—some kind of nut house?' Rafe shouted. 'I tell you, by godfreys, I'm gittin' out of here!' With a week's growth of whiskers and his hair every whichway it was no wonder Bunny, blanching, hastily backed out of reach.

'I'll fetch Daddy,' she said, hand on the door.

'You fetch my horse an' git my clothes or I'm bustin' outa here just like I am!' he yelled, shoving up, and Bunny left on the run.

Looked like that ought to do it, he thought, settling back. You have to take a firm hand with these conniving Yankees, let them know where you stood, or they would steal the fillings right out of your teeth. There was just one thing they couldn't face up to—being made to look a fool. No matter how big they got if you could get the laugh on them—or make 'em think you were going to—you could jump them through hoops and make them turn handflips. They were as leery of ridicule as a bunch of cow critters on the move was to lightning.

This was Rafe's cherished conviction, but as the half hours dragged by and the sun began climbing ever nearer to high noon it became apparent that, in Bunny, he'd met a different breed of cat. Scowling, furious, he grabbed up the stool and commenced hammering the wall with it, punctuating this clamor with some pretty inflamable language.

When ten minutes of this brought nothing but a flock of frogs into his throat he decided if he was ever to get out of here it was time he was putting his crazy threat into action. He jumped out of bed, flung down the stool and, wrapped in a sheet, strode seething to the door. Yanking it furiously open he stopped with dropped jaw.

Bunny sat in a rocker less than three yards away with a double barreled shotgun pointed square at him. She wasn't smiling, either. She looked as though for half a cent she would just as lief pull both triggers.

Rafe clutched his sheet, swallowing uncomfortably. With that look in her eye it didn't seem the most propitious moment to assume any further hostilities. By way of temporizing he said, 'Maybe I better *habla* with your father.' He waited and when she still didn't speak, he said with a feeble attempt at a smile, 'Might be a good idea if you called him.'

'You've got plenty of wind. Try calling him yourself.'

There was something about the way she said it that told him plain he'd be wasting his breath. He took a careful squint, had to grudgingly admit she was a heap better looking than a Yank had any right to be. Slim as a willow-busty, too. Pansy eyes that could turn dark and deep as mountain pools. You'd never think a girl young and lovely as her could be so durn feisty!

He shifted weight with considerable care. 'I wisht you'd put that scattergun down, ma'am—'

'If it makes you nervous, close the door.'

'How'm I goin' to talk with the door closed?'

She kept the gun where it was. It was plain he wasn't getting anywhere at all. Perhaps it was time to try a little sugar coating. 'Seems a shame, daggone it, a nice young filly purty as you be—'

'I've been flattered by experts,' Bunny said, with her lip curled. 'Why don't you get back in bed and behave yourself? Daddy knows what's best. If you really want to be up and about, the quickest way would be to do as you're told. We'd be remiss in our duty—'

'Duty!' Rafe bleated.

'After all, a county coroner, you know, has certain obliga—'

'Coroner!' Rafe shouted. 'Do I look *dead!*'

She studied him a while, red lips trembling, almost breaking into a smile. 'If you could only see yourself. I'll tell you the truth. You look mad as a hatter. There! You see? Daddy's right. You look positively rabid; if he was to turn you loose we'd never hear the end of it.'

Rafe did look pretty wild for a fact.

Trouble was that stage-robbing bunch he'd fell in with back yonder had passed away the time with some pretty weird tales of what could happen to caught Confederates who got off the straight and narrow or come broadside to the notions of one of these blue-nosed little Caesars.

Bunny pushed a dangle of hair off her cheek. 'I'm afraid there's no help for it. You'll have to be kept under observation for at least a couple of weeks—that's the law. I suppose,' she said brightly, 'we *could* get a few of the preliminaries disposed of.'

'Pre-preliminaries?'

'All those terrible forms. You've no idea the number of questions—town, county, the Territory and federal government—it takes most of Daddy's time just getting the papers filed. If you'll get back in bed, I can fix you some lunch. My arms are getting awfully cramped.'

Rafe, so tangled in imaginings by now he hardly knew whether to cuss or shriek, someway managed to get himself turned around and, still clutched to the sheet, like a drowning man stumbled back to the bed and let himself down.

One thing got through the whirl of his thoughts, that lunch she had mentioned. If he could hang on for that, and give the impression he was so wore out she'd put that damned artillery up, he might—just might—get loose from this yet. He wriggled out of the sheet and, hearing her step, lay back with a groan, dragging it up over him clear to the chin.

She did not immediately appear, however. When she did come in she had a pad and a pencil; the sawed-off Greener had been left behind. She sat down near the door and said, pencil poised, 'Your full name, please.'

'Rafe—Rafe Bender.' He'd been minded to give her some made-up monicker and was a little surprised to find he'd stuck to the truth. She looked a little strange, too. Her mouth was partway open. But she wrote it down, then said crisply, 'Date and place of birth, father's name, maiden name of mother, names and ages of brothers and sisters.'

When she'd put that all down she was silent for a spell, apparently considering, the cut of her stare seeming queerer than ever. At last with a sigh she passed on to army experience, rank and outfit, a couple of dozen other things, finally asking the date of his discharge. If she missed anything Rafe wasn't aware of it.

He felt about as public as a zebra in a fish pond. Despite his pretentions to complete cooperation and the need he'd seen to butter her up, resentment made him testily say, 'If your old man during the war was such a comfort to Grant how come the people round here ain't beat no path to his door?'

'Please?'

He said, 'How come all the quiet? Don't he see no one here?'

'Oh, he does most of his work at the office. As County Health Officer and Coroner he has a place at the courthouse next door to the sheriff. Actually he doesn't really practice much now, only accepting professionally those cases which interest him personally.'

'The well-heeled ones, I reckon,' Rafe

said.

Bunny looked at him reproachfully. 'You don't understand. Daddy isn't at all well. He can't hardly stand the sight—he saw so many horrible—'

'Kinda tender in his mind, huh?'

'You were in the war.' She said defensively, 'You know the kind of things he had to do without anesthetics, half the time without proper medicines. He came out here to forget—'

'And when that didn't work he took to hittin' the bottle,' Rafe said, warming up to it. 'Sure, I know, he had it rough. He *looks* like he did!'

She looked shocked, and then indignant. She came out of the chair with her eyes like daggers and, with her cheeks white and stiff, marched out of the room, pausing only to slam the door shut behind her.

CHAPTER THREE

Rafe, somewhat abashed though not honestly ashamed, rather nervously wondered if she'd gone after that twin-barreled field piece. When after several moments she hadn't reappeared he cautiously let the rest of his breath out. If he was going to build a dust now was certainly the time to get started. With the sheet gathered round him he slipped over to the door.

After standing for a bit with his ear squeezed against it he caught a series of thumps, the bang of a stovelid, followed by the clatter of tinware and china. Fixing lunch he decided, and eased the door open.

He saw an oilcloth-covered table, another God Bless sampler, four chairs primly lined up in front of the wall beneath it. He guessed this was where they generally put on the feed bags, and moved out a step to scan the rest of the room. Straightaway he saw all washed and ironed, carefully folded on the seat of a horsehair sofa, his missing clothes; his disreputable hat was on the floor nearby, along with his runover boots and scuffed shell belt. Vastly relieved he scooped them up and lost no time getting back to the girl's room where he clapped on his hat, stomped into the boots, and hurriedly flung on the rest of his outfit.

Beaded with sweat from so much exertion he stood there a moment, hanging onto the wall, waiting for things to settle back into focus. Being down on his back had sure taken it out of him. He got his gun belt around him and buckled it. He still felt a little woozy, but he daren't let that stand in his way now. Out of habit he slipped the Walker Colt from its holster, checked the mechanism, replaced the loads from the loops of his belt and moved to the window.

Pouching the big pistol he sleeved the sweat off his cheeks. The upper half of the window was open but, shaking like he was, the acrobatics involved in such a mode of departure required more faith than Rafe could summon. He got the upper sash back where it belonged and, gasping for breath, was about to tackle the lower when he heard Bunny's step making straight for the door.

He'd have given something then to have been safe back in bed; but this, of course, was out of the question. With a muttered curse he flung up the screeching sash, threw a leg across the sill, squeezed hatted head and chest through and, frantically hauling the other leg up, levered himself out.

It wasn't much of a drop but he lit all spraddled like a shotgunned duck. Bunny's startled cry jerked him back to the realities. He got himself up and stumbled toward a corner of the house, half falling round it. Directly before him was a shed built of shakes from which an inquiring whinny lent him the additional strength to find the door and drag it open. Bathsheba, his black-and-white spotted mare, sidled around with an impatient nicker.

Rafe found his brass-horned brush-scarred saddle, carbine still in the boot, and got it on her. Gagging for breath, scared to waste further time in a hunt for his bridle, he scrambled aboard, banged her ribs with his heels, and lit out like hell emigrating on cart wheels.

As he peered over his shoulder Bunny, her arms waving wildly, burst from the house. What she called was lost behind the rush of the wind. Something flashed in her hand that looked like his spurs, but he wasn't going back—not for all the tea in China. He jerked his face to the front. Still using his heels, he caught a glimpse of peaked roofs and tall false fronts poking up from scrub oak maybe half a mile ahead. And right in his path, coming down the road, was a horse and buggy—Pike on the seat.

The girl's father, shouting, made a grab for the whip.

Leaning wide for the turn, left hand locked in her mane, Rafe kneed Bathsheba hard around and sent her snorting through the crackle of brush.

'Hold on, you fool!' Pike yelled, standing up; but Rafe had had all of their care he could stomach. He might not be showing the right sort of spirit, but he meant to get clear of that pair if it killed him. Ducking into the guard of his arms he kept going, booting the mare harder every time she hit ground.

He reckoned they must have made a rare sight popping up and down through the whip of that brush. He suspected he was lucky

Pike hadn't a rifle. Enraged at the thwarting of so much endeavor there was no telling what a damn Yankee might do.

A quarter mile farther on Rafe came out of the brush on the flank of a ridge. Peering back he saw no evidence of pursuit. The only dust he could spot was ballooning up through the trees back in the neighborhood of the house he'd escaped from. He reckoned that was Pike rushing home to see about Bunny.

It came over him then if he meant to slip into Dry Bottom at all he'd never have a better chance. It was dollars to doughnuts, once Red Nose got back, every able-bodied gent in reach would be put to beating the brush to retake him—they might even send for the soldiers! There wasn't nothing a Yank wouldn't do to skin a Rebel!

Just the same Rafe kept on without slacking off till he'd crossed the hump and worked far enough down along the far slope to make sure any change in direction was covered.

'Whew!' he gasped, pulling up, all a-tremble.

He sure enough felt like he'd been hauled through a hornput. He wasn't scairt so much at the old boozer himself as he was of what Pike stood for, those damned two-legged vultures, greed and skulduggery, that was standing so much of the South on her beam ends. Maybe if they hadn't killed Lincoln things might have been different. But the way it stacked up with Grant in the White House and them tycoons at him every hour of the night, any pore misguided Rebel that had enough savvy to punch sand down a rat hole would go to almost any lengths to keep himself clear of the blue-bellied skunks that had got themselves put in charge of this country.

He thought of Bunny again. He plain couldn't help it, but that didn't mean he didn't know better. There was things about a diamondback a feller could admre, but that didn't signify he figured to get in bed with one! If she hadn't been a Yankee—but she was, no getting around it.

He followed the line of the ridge due north till he arrived at an outcrop thatched with juniper and, through the branches, saw the town's roofs spread out below him. Didn't look too much. Wasn't even built around a plaza. Just a single dirt street with some lanes straggling off it; hardly bigger, he thought, than Flat Rock, Kentucky, even if it was a county seat town—he could take her word for that, anyhow. If he ever was to get reunited with his folks, county seat towns was the likeliest to hear of them.

So he had to go in, no matter what Pike had got up his sleeve. Today was a Saturday, best time of all. Be some risky asking questions but at least, this being a market day, he wasn't so like to be the only stray cat.

He eased Bathsheba onto the grade, letting her pick her own way. She'd been raised in the mountains and could wheel on a dime and, though she mightn't look it, she had a heap of speed. Her pappy had been a Billy horse, according to what that breed had told him, and everybody knew Billy horses was fast. Short coupled, long underneath, plenty of muscles inside and out. Hadn't been for all that hair on her legs and that broomy tail with the burrs matted into it some Yank would have stole her long before this.

Dry Bottom, seen up close when he got into it was even less impressive than it had been from the ridge. Marple's Mercantile, aside from the courthouse, took up more room than anything else. It was housed in a huge rambling barn of a place, and next on the right was the Bon Ton Cafe, then a harness shop, gunsmith, a pool hall and barber. On the other side was the courthouse, two-storied, all the second floor windows having bars across them. The next lot was vacant, grown to tin cans and weeds. On the far side of this was what had all the earmarks of being a honkytonk. Foot high letters across its front said: COW PALACE—Jack Dahl, Prop.

This Bathsheba was a real knowing mare,

ever alert to Rafe's best interests. She'd spotted this joint even quicker than he had and, ears cocked, stopped short, one eye rolling back to see how he was taking it.

As a matter of fact he was still peering round. The next structure beyond housed a hat shop and baker, and after that was the bank, double-storied and brick as befitted so established a place in the community. The whole last block on that side was taken up with a feed yard and livery, the poorer homes spreading out to the south, tiny islands of junk among the cholla and greasewood topped by an occasional flowering saguaro. The more affluent had their residences on the lanes feeding off the main drag.

Bathsheba pawed impatiently. Thus reminded, Rafe hitched up a leg and got down. He sure didn't like to spoil her this way but there wasn't much choice if you were hunting information. Her last owner must have been a sure-enough scholar because if a man didn't take a firm hand with her she'd haul up in front of every grog shop in sight.

Rasping his jaw with a wistful look in the direction of the barber's pole Rafe reached around to catch hold of the reins, only then recollecting the loss of his bridle. 'Well, hell,' he said and, ducking under the rail, pushed through the bat wings into Jack Dahl's.

If mirrors and mahogany and naked

females on canvas was any measure of prosperity this Cow Palace, Rafe decided, must be a mighty source of comfort to all who had a stake in it. Though it wasn't precisely packed right now it was doing all right for the middle of the day. The faro layout, cage and wheel, and even the blackjack table had customers, and a mob three deep was bellied up to the bar. Evidently, and plainly not too far away, there were mines in production to judge by the Cousin Jacks jostling elbows with the teamsters and cowhands milling about a roped-off twenty-foot square of dance floor perspiring and noisy as a sackful of frogs.

Tobacco smoke swirled in blue layers below the bright flare of the Rochester lamps which apparently were worked day and night in this dive. In constant circulation a bevy of cuties in spangles were hustling to separate the boys from their wages. There was a sudden scramble for the arena as a three-piece band swung into the rollicking strains of *Soldiers Joy*.

Near as sudden as it started, and before Rafe had latched hold of someone he could talk to, the music went sour and splintered off into dischord. Following the startled sweep of eyes doorward Rafe saw framed in the bat wings the longnosed freckled face of Bathsheba. With her lip peeling back she threw her head up and nickered.

The cowhands guffawed hilariously, clouting each other and hooting and hollering. A heavy-set gent in gray derby and striped leg-clutching pants got redfaced out of his chair at the poker game, went stomping past Rafe with his mouth whitely clamped about a stump of black cheroot. Like a prodded bull with his eye on the muleta came a beetle-browed bouncer and a third burly specimen, getting shed of his apron, came hotfooting out from the bar with a bungstarter just as Bathsheba pushed in through the doors.

Rafe stuck out a leg. Beetle Brows, loping into it, hit the floor spraddled out and cleaned a swath through the sawdust three foot long with his chin. The cowpunchers, hooting, liked to laugh their fool heads off. Bathsheba, after the fashion of one not entirely sure of her welcome, came timidly in. The guy in the derby waved his arms, started swearing. The barman ran up waving his bung starter. Bathsheba rolled her eyes and whinnied. The bartender said, 'She's slipped her headstall—'

'Never mind that—get her out!' shouted Dahl, brandishing his derby and sure enough seeming about fit to be tied.

The bouncer, a little glazed in his expression, with a knee drawn under him appeared to be trying to get himself up. The feller who had took off his apron was sidling around with one arm stuck out, it being difficult to tell if he were trying to catch the mare or only keep from being stepped on. There wasn't much doubt what Bathsheba thought about it. Stretching out her neck she showed him both sets of teeth.

The barkeep jumped back. The crowd roared and hooted. Dahl cried furiously, 'Who's the owner of this monstrosity?' and Rafe didn't know whether to speak out or not. He figured a lot could be said on both sides of the question; but when the beetle-browed bouncer, still on one knee, commenced to fumble a hip pocket, Rafe didn't have much choice. He sent the bugger sliding with a well directed boot.

Dahl and the barkeep both of them livid, converged on him threateningly. From someplace Dahl produced a sock filled with shot. The barkeep, glowering, lifted his bung starter.

'Now, just a minute—' Rafe said, nervous.

'Get her out,' Dahl said, 'and get 'er out quick!'

Rafe said uncomfortably, 'Bathsheba's kind of notional. She—'

'You got thirty seconds!' Dahl sounded half strangled.

The mare, watching Rafe, began to look a little reproachful. 'Go on, you!' the barkeep growled, flourishing his bung starter. He cut around, moving nearer. The mare showed the whites of her eyes.

'Look out,' Rafe warned. 'No tellin' what she'll do if you excite her.'

Mr. Dahl said viciously, 'You puttin' her out or ain't you?'

Rafe, tired of being shoved, yelled, 'No!' and Jack Dahl stopped in his tracks.

He took a long look at Rafe and, beckoning up two more of his hirelings, spat out his cigar. 'Take 'em, boys,' he grunted, and closed in behind to give them a hand.

The barkeep made a wicked pass with his bung starter. Rafe, sliding under it, put a boot against his belly and the barkeep's wind went out with a mighty *whoosh*, Bathsheba, ears flattened, began backing toward the bar, the crowd at that end making haste to move elsewhere. Rafe, as though reluctant, backed off some himself.

Beetle Brows, on his feet again, cracked an ugly grin. He had a gun in his fist—a short-barreled pocket pistol, and it seemed fairly well established he intended to use it. Dahl and the other pair, scrinch eyed and malevolent, were stepping farther apart to come in on the flanks.

'Look,' Rafe grumbled, 'I'm peaceful as hell when I'm left alone, but if you're goin' to play rough I won't be responsible.' He shook an admonitory finger under Dahl's nose. 'You fellers keep on—'

'And you'll do what?' Dahl said with his

lip curled.

'Just remember,' Rafe told them, 'you been warned.'

Now Dahl was a man who had considerable pride. He had moved to Dry Bottom with a number of his friends who'd been in on that Jayhawking business along the Kansas border. He liked to be thought a pretty tough cookie; and besides all this the place was packed with galoots he needed to impress, hardrock men and rough playing cowpokes, all watching with grins and filling the ozone with cheap advice. He couldn't afford to back down—not even if this drifter proved more fruity than he looked.

Dahl tugged an end of his black moustache, swung a hard look around and fetched up his chin. The barkeep took a fresh grip on his bung starter. Beetle Brows' grin, above the snub-nosed pistol, spread in pleased anticipation. The other pair, grunting, spat on their hands and then, all together, the whole push moved in.

The gaunt stranger, sighing, looked extremely reluctant—everybody afterward, agreed on that much. Some claimed he never actually moved so much as a finger until the barkeep's bung starter whacked against the mare.

Then everything seemed to happen at once. The Rebel's left boot, sailing up out of nowhere, took the barkeep under the jaw like a ball bat. He stretched six inches and went out like a light. Nobody saw the stranger reach for his iron, but suddenly the glint of it was slicing through the tangle like the knives of a dozen Injuns. It went *whunk* against something and Beetle Brows, without even time to let go of his pistol, popped out of the melee like he'd been shot from a cannon. Arms flailing wildly he went down with a thump, blood on his face, shirt hanging down like a tatter of doll rags. Bathsheba, with her head tucked between front legs, was kicking hell out of the bar when another of Dahl's bruisers went slamming head first into a wall and kind of wilted.

Dahl shook like the steam had run out of him, but only for a moment. Red necked and livid, he yelled in a fury, 'No secesh bastard that ever was foaled—'

Rafe's gun started pounding. When it quit all those beautiful mirrors plus a sizeable number of stacked bottles and glasses were in shards on the floor and Dahl's eyes looked like they'd roll off his cheekbones.

'This has gone far enough,' a new voice said crisply. A frock-coated gent in a stovepipe hat, whiskers curling out of his jowls like piano wires, pushed from the crowd to stop by Dahl's elbow. Even Bathsheba left off what she was doing as, avidly silent, all heads swung to watch. In his rusty garb of the backwoods politician he didn't look like a man who had this town in his pocket, yet he certainly had everybody's attention.

Dahl looked about ready to call out the troops. He was so mad he was shaking, but the other said coolly, 'Better let it drop,' and, skewered by that unwinking regard, the Cow Palace's proprietor managed after a fashion to get hold of himself.

He was still swelled up like a poisoned pup, the red from his neck surging into his cheeks. 'Very well, Mr. Chilton,' he said, like it choked him, 'but who's going to pay for all that smashed glass and bar?'

A soft pale hand rasped the mutton-chop whiskers. 'It can probably be arranged for some of the loss to be written off.' Chilton's cold eyes scaled Rafe in shrewd appraisal. 'Do you always react with such violence to stimulants?'

'Depends,' Rafe said, 'on the stimulant.'

Chilton smiled through his teeth. 'Would you be interested in a job?'

'We-ell, I wouldn't figure to put no widows and children out on the street.'

'Oh, it's nothing like that,' Chilton declared. 'I, ah, notice your mare has no bridle—she a cutter?'

'She's cut a few in her time.'

'I suppose,' Chilton said, 'you're familiar with cattle.'

'I been around 'em some,' Rafe admitted.

'You got cows you want moved?'

'Not exactly. I need somebody who can manage a ranch, only it isn't that simple,' Chilton said, looking thoughtful. 'If you'd care to step over to my office—' His fishbelly glance, shuttling across Dahl and his goggling understrappers, took on a trace of impatience. 'I expect I can dig up enough solid facts...'

Rafe, having also noticed their looks, cut in, 'I'm persuaded for that, suh. But my old pappy always told me the first rule of business is to know who you're dealing with.'

'Tsk, tsk—of course. I'm so in the habit of everyone—' Clucking again, he pushed out his chest. 'Alph Chilton at your service, president and general manager of the People's Bank & Trust. Capital assets eight hundred and fifty-four thousand, surplus one hundred—'

'Proud to meet up with you,' Rafe said heartily, grabbing the pale hand and vigorously pumping it. 'Just Rafe, here. Not much surplus but ample room for improvement as the feller said.'

The banker, wincing, extricated his hand. Flexing it a moment, and apparently reassured, he said, 'I must be getting back, but if you'll step over for a moment I feel certain we can arrive at a profitable arrangement.' That last he pushed out with considerable unction, not smiling exactly, but nevertheless managing to give the impression of an unending jingle of cascading dollars all bound for Rafe's pockets.

★   ★   ★

The bank was the only brick building in town. Lines of jostling people, all with money in their paws, stood before the tellers' cages in an ornate lobby replete with guards and grilles and an over-abundance of stuffed animal and bird heads; and the pride of them all, a dusty bald eagle, hovered on spread wings above the door to Chilton's office.

The banker escorted Rafe past the gun hung lackies, herded him inside and got him ensconsed in a leather-covered chair that sort of closed out the world's woes like the sweet scented arms of a harem houri.

Chilton, after removing his hat, pushed a box of fat cigars across the shine of his desk and then, while his guest was stowing away half a dozen, fetched out a bottle of fine bourbon and a pair of glasses.

Rafe, surreptitiously pinching himself, picked up the pushed-forward nearest. Cold eyes sparkling above the rim of his lifted own, Chilton proposed, 'Your health, young feller, and all that goes with it.'

Rafe smacked his lips and, feeling some stronger, gawped around like a bumpkin.

The banker evidently lived about as high off the hog as a man in this country was liable to get. Recognition of this brought to mind an old saw having to do with gifts and Greeks. With that jaw, and eyes that would have looked as much to home in one of those moose heads, Chilton's red carpet welcome had a lot more behind it than was being tossed onto the table.

With the stiff-fingered hand Rafe set down his glass. 'Not much point chasin' clean around the barn, eh?'

The banker, showing his store teeth, sat back while Rafe fired up. Then he said, leaning forward, 'This property I mentioned is being let go to hell. A man's entitled to protect his investment.'

'No argument there. Your bank owns the property?'

'Bank holds the mortgage. Last payment made—and it took care only of interest—was more than a year ago. These payments,' Chilton explained, 'are due quarterly. Our depositors have—'

'I dunno,' Rafe said. 'If you're wantin' 'em forclosed I'd say your best bet's the sheriff.'

Chilton snorted. 'He won't even go near the place, and his deputy's more scairt of Spangler than he is. To make a long story short what we've got out there is a bunch of damn fools, a family of wastrels. The old man knows stock and that's all you can say for them. Left alone I expect he could make a real go of it—that's why we loaned him the money. But—'

'How much was that?'

'Thirty thousand.'

Rafe whistled. 'That spread must take up half the county.'

'Takes up enough. An old Spanish grant. First couple of years we didn't have no trouble. Then they took on this Spangler—'

'Who's he?' Rafe cut in.

'Foreman, range boss, whatever you want to call him. I won't try to fool you, He's a plenty rough customer. Old man's been failing—eyes ain't what they used to be. He's fell into the habit of letting Spangler pretty much run things. Spangler's stealing him blind.'

Rafe said, 'Where do I come in?'

'I don't say it'll be easy; you'll earn every nickel you're going to get out of this.' Chilton said confidentially, 'You'll be going out there as the bank's representative. You'll look into these losses, do whatever you think's called for.'

'Hmmm,' Rafe said dubiously.

'You'll draw two hundred a month, and a thousand dollar bonus if you wind this up to the bank's satisfaction. That's a lot of money, mister.'

It was a good deal more than Rafe had ever got hold of or ever expected to. 'This

Spangler,' he said, 'must be hell on wheels.' He got up with a sigh.

'Where you going?' Chilton growled.

'Ain't much doubt where I'd go if I took on that chore.'

'You don't have to fire him, if that's what's bothering you. I'm not tying your hands. Work under cover, do it any way you want. There's a girl out there, old man's daughter, wild as a hare.' Chilton smiled suggestively.

'I guess not,' Rafe said, turning to hide the black leap of his anger.

'Where else can a secesh make that kind of money?'

The banker had something there, but money wasn't everything. Rafe, arriving at the door, grabbed hold of the knob. Chilton said, 'Figure you can afford to entertain such fine sentiments?'

Rafe, chewing his lip, glared over a shoulder. 'What's that supposed to mean?'

'Got the price of that damage you inflicted across the street?'

Rafe bristled. 'An' if I haven't?'

'Better think over my offer if you don't want to find yourself headed for Yuma.'

Rafe had heard enough about this Arizona country to understand there was mighty little hope for anyone sent there. The Territorial Prison was about all there was to Yuma, and a lot more went there than ever got out. He didn't doubt for an instant Chilton had enough influence to get him committed. Pike was on his mind, too.

The banker showed his dentures. 'When a man works for me I take care of him. Now what are you going to do?'

'I don't see that I got much choice,' Rafe said bitterly.

CHAPTER FOUR

The sun, dropping rapidly, was near submerged in reefs of copper cloud stretching mile on mile above the western rim of sight when Rafe, aboard the skewbald, some hours later moved out of a draw and began climbing east through a straggle of stunted juniper and pear. Six weeks grass was the color of straw and hardly came higher than the mare's shaggy pasterns. Directly ahead were the dark scarps of a peak that stood up butter-like straight as a rifle, fiercely red where the light broke across a patchwork of shadows going all the way from pale blue to black. Beyond, shoved up like slabs of gray slate, loomed the spires of the Cherrycows.

Only the mare's shod hoofs and the occasional chirp of a startled bird broke the land's heavy silence that seemed laid up like stones. The brooding quiet held an eerie resentment Rafe could almost taste and there was in him suddenly a feeling of doors being closed just ahead of him.

A wild and lonesome country, hard to get into and probably harder to get out of if the folks who lived here took a dislike to him, which they very well might if the word got around he was repping for Chilton.

More and more he was tempted to chuck it and run—but run where? And if he did get away what then of the quest that had hauled him half across a continent? Didn't he owe it to his folks to come up with them?

Of course, he'd no real proof they'd ever been in this region. The Old Man never had cottoned to cattle; in a land big as this he'd surely go into horses, or hogs maybe. Or would stubbornness have kept him back of a plow?

A lot of that stubbornness was in Rafe, too. He despised, after putting his shoulder to a wheel, to let it get away from him. Cross-grained as a mule, his old pappy had called him, and it was a heap kinder language than some of the descriptions other folks had flung after him.

Rafe sighed. A powerful lot of water had gone rolling under the bridges since that day he'd quit the Ozarks to join up with the boys in gray. Been a mighty mort of changes.

He guessed a man ought to look for the good in things. He reckoned he wouldn't of been so down on this chore if that banker hadn't told him a girl was tied into it. Danger was something you could learn to run elbows with; but if there was any one thing could really tear a man up it was a woman every time!

He had generally figured to fight clear of them. The times he hadn't was sharp in his head as any memory he'd hung onto. And twice as loud. He could still see the wide-open eyes of that Pike filly peering blue as larkspur across the ugly look of that Greener. And here he was, crowding his luck like any half-baked Boston, a-humping and a-hustling to cram himself neck deep in a deal where Hoyle and logic went straight out the window and the rules, if any, was built to drag smiles from some addlebrained female!

That was what Rafe thought.

'I ought to be bored for the simples!' he snarled, and hauled up Bathsheba in a slash of wild cursing. Any guy not ready for a string of spools should be able to see what that banker was up to with a woman in the game and the stakes big as these was. All Chilton had to do was set back and wait till Rafe or some other mushhead like him got the skids knocked out from under that foreman. He wouldn't even have to shake the dang tree! Just flatter the girl or threaten foreclosure and the whole shebang would fall right in his lap!

Rafe scowled something awful, thinking he ought to cut his string, too proud to whip out his knife to do it. He had a nagging hunch he was plumb on the threshold of times so parlous they could lose a man every tooth in his head, then beat him over the butt with a broomstick. Women and Yankees! Goddlemighty!

Yet to run in blind panic wouldn't help a heap, either. Not knowing the country how far would he get up against guys like Pike and that conniving dang banker? Both of 'em pecking more pull, probably, than a twenty-mule borax team!

Pride was fine, but it made a poor supher. Why, he didn't even *know* these crazy dang people! No skin off *his* nose if, after he got this Spangler off their backs, Chilton shoved 'em right out in the catclaw. Nobody'd appointed Rafe Bender their keeper!

Though he'd never admit it, Rafe, deep down, was a pretty decent sort. He might stick up a stage when the going got rough, even whittle a steak off somebody's cow, but the kind of deal Alph Chilton was up to looked a pretty hard thing for a man to have to live with. Mighty near bad as skinning a orphan. About as low down as a feller could get.

The whole thing gave him a kind of mental indigestion, fetching his convictions up so harsh against his needs. He didn't have to be told he was in a real bind, and he was no more anxious to get the dirt spaded over him than anybody else. A Johnny Reb could find himself powerful quick dead playing ticktacktoe with these greedy Yank carpetbaggers.

Rafe growled and swore and sighed again. Trying to be a Christian was sure as hell a full-time job! Everybody these days was looking out for Number One. If a gent wasn't able to blow his own nose he'd likely wait a long time for someone else to do it.

He kneed Bathsheba up the trail. Juniper fled into scrub oak and piñon. Grass clumps began to show among the pear and Spanish bayonet and the land leveled off into rolling swells. Prairie chickens thrummed out of the thickets. A road-runner scuttled through the grain heavy stems of green-bladed feed and the mare came into a meadow that was just like something straight out of a dream.

Despite Alph Chilton's detailed directions Rafe could hardly believe this oasis was real. Just like in McGuffy's Reader! Green stretching every place. The soft gurgle of water drew his glance to the creek and Bathsheba, impatient, broke through a trembling screen of willows and, wading into the flow, put her head down to drink.

Rafe put together a smoke. Must be close onto forty acres, and alfalfa at that! Pulling the good smell of it deep inside him he dragged the quirly across his tongue, firing up. There hadn't been such a sight since old Jim Wolf lost his pants in a snowdrift.

Off yonder the tops of a dozen great cottonwoods threshed in the breeze whipping down off the mountains. The whirling blades of a mill fetched his look to the flat roofs of buildings over beyond a far tangle of pens.

He reckoned this layout was the sure-enough headquarters of the old Ortega grant—Gourd and Vine they was calling it now according to what Alph Chilton had told him. A hundred thousand unfenced acres. There had been more but a heap had gone into Ortega marryings and then, in bad times, considerable more had been sold. How this crop of gringos had got hold of it wasn't quite clear.

In fact, now Rafe came to think back, there seemed quite a pile of things the banker hadn't gone into. The only name dropped into their talk had been that of Spangler, the bullypuss range boss Chilton claimed was stealing them blind. Nor had the banker explained how he came to have a lien.

Increasingly uneasy, Rafe watched a rider quit the maze of pens and, circling the buildings, come on at a lope. Pitching aside the remains of his smoke Rafe eased Bathsheba up out of the creek. If that feller hadn't seen him before he certain sure did when Rafe came out of the trees.

Rafe's eyes suddenly narrowed. This galoot coming toward him looked almighty like the slab-sided bustard who'd been leading that bunch Rafe had tried to flag down before he'd wound up in the hands of Grant's bone setter.

The nearer he come the more like him he seemed. Rafe was pretty hard put to keep a rein on his temper. It didn't help none when this guy, even before he'd pulled up, yelled, 'What the hell do you think you're doin'?'

His voice was rough as the look on his face. He was big, heavy-set, with great slabs for hands. His chaps-covered legs appeared thick as fence posts. Menace and suspicion peered through slitted eyes as he set up his horse in a slather of grit. 'When I ask a man somethin' he damn well better answer!'

Rafe, with both hands over the knob of his saddle, said, 'I'm huntin' a job—'

'And I'm a Chinaman's uncle!'

Rafe wasn't going to take issue on that, though he thought to himself the guy looked more like a chimp with his long fat nose and stringy mustache staggling over that steel-trap slit of a mouth. Even his ears stuck out like an ape's and his winkless, red-veined eyes were about as readable as rock. He was certainly a beauty.

This guy said, like he was talking to a fool,

'I guess you don't believe in signs. I guess you're one of them as has to be showed—'

'What signs?' Rafe said, and Frozenface got right up in his stirrups like he was more than some minded to take bodily hold of him. Before he could do so another voice said, 'What you got there, Jess?'

Frozenface, never for an instant taking his look off Rafe, growled, 'Another damn drifter! It's gettin' so a man can't put a foot out of doors without stumblin' over some goddamn saddle bum! I say it's time, by Gawd, we was stringin' up a few!'

'You know the old man wouldn't hold still for that—'

'Who's to tell? A guy with a choke strap round his neck ain't—'

'We don't have to do that. Take his stuff, put him afoot and haze him off into the dunes like you done the rest of them,' the newcomer said; and something about the sound, some inflection of his voice, pulled Rafe's face about.

His jaw fell open. *'Duck!'* he cried with his eyes lighting up, and would have sent Bathsheba straight away over except that, before he could do it, a gun snout jabbed hard against his ribs. A gate-hinge growl advised, 'Set right still if you don't want them guts blowed hell west an' crooked!'

In the whirl and churn of Rafe's confused thoughts there was just enough savvy to understand he was about as close to planting as a man could come and still keep breathing. This dark faced Jess, if that order were ignored, wouldn't hesitate a minute. It was more reflex, however, than any conscious intention that caused Rafe's legs to lock the mare in her tracks. His glance stayed riveted on the handsome dandy in the bottle-green coat, stock and tall beaver hat who, in white cheeked dismay, stared incredulously back.

Chagrin—almost a sickness—peered out of that weasel-like handsome face. Consternation crept into the bloodless look of it, and a wildness sprang into the fright-widened eyes as Rafe said, 'Hell, don't you know your own brother?'

The man glared back, rebelliously shaking his head. He licked his lips and tried to pull himself together. 'I have no brother.'

'Mean to say you ain't Duke Bender?'

An ugly red flamed up through the other's face. His cheeks became mottled and he said, thick with fury, 'I'm Bender, all right—'

'You never had no brother Rafe?'

The man said harshly, 'He was killed in the war.'

Rafe just looked at him. Slowly his lip curled, seeing the hate and shame in that face, the trembling fright. 'By God, you'd like to believe that, wouldn't you!'

Bender bristled. 'I don't know what your

game is, feller, but you sure as hell ain't no brother of mine. Rafe was killed in the war. We got a paper to prove it!'

CHAPTER FIVE

Rafe sat there numbly trying to figure this out. They maybe did have a paper; it wouldn't be the first time mistakes of that nature had been made during the confusions of fighting a war. But the scared incredulity of Duke's first look was still bright in front of him, making a mockery of all that had been said. Duke recognized him sure as hell; and there was one more thing you couldn't hardly get around: his brother didn't want Rafe climbing out of no grave to stand between him and what he figured he had coming when the Old Man went.

It made Rafe pretty sick. Back on the farm he'd found excuses for the boy, ways of glossing over, covering up the things he'd done, knowing Duke wasn't bad, only thinner-skinned than most, too quick to lay hold of notions that pleased him, a sight too gullible, too easy steered.

He'd always been one to find the shortest way out when things began to bog up. Aside from his folks nobody ever, back home, had called him anything but 'Duck'—which had sure used to make Rafe Bender boil.

He sighed, thinking back, seeing how they had spoiled him, never making the boy face up to his problems. Now the boy was a man, still hugging kids' notions, still bound and determined every guy and his uncle was out of step but him. It made a pretty ugly picture.

'Well ...' Spangler said when nobody else seemed minded to speak, 'I reckon that settles that.' He flashed Rafe a hard grin. 'You heard him. Git down.'

Rafe looked at his brother. 'We'll hear what Maw has to say on the subject.'
He'd been prepared for Duke's sneer but not for the venom, the cold slashing scorn that came out of Duke's voice like a whip when he said, 'If you was Rafe you'd of damn well knowed better'n that!'

'Maw ...' Dread climbed into Rafe's throat. 'You—you mean Maw's—' He couldn't bring the word out.

'Rafe,' Duke said, like it was purest gospel, 'put the coffin together and help me bury her!'

Rafe's jaw fell open. He sat there too shocked, too bewildered by so bald-faced a lie, to do more than goggle. And he was still hard at it when Duke in a kind of choked voice snarled, 'Get rid of him!' and, whirling his mount, spurred off like he couldn't get out of sight quick enough.

'All right, you,' Spangler said, crowding his horse up against Bathsheba. 'You comin' outa that saddle or hev I—'

Rafe, mild as milk and with his mind, by the look, caught up in some backwash of painful memories, pushed out his crippled paw in a kind of feeble protest. Being Rafe's right hand it naturally drew Spangler's notice, his sharpened interest showing in the relaxing of his muscles as his stare took in the uselessness of stiffened clawlike fingers.

'I reckon not,' Rafe murmured, his drawl gone cold as froglegs; and only then, too late, did the Bender range boss spy the swift-enlargening barrel of the gun coming at him like a bat out of Carlsbad in the stranger's other fist. Cursing, he tried, but there was no time left to get his head out of the way. He went out of the saddle like a shotgunned duck.

★   ★   ★

Built in the days when the danger of Apaches was a very real and ever present pearl, the Ortega Grant headquarters looked not unlike a fort. Constructed of sun-baked adobes, the buildings were laid out in the form of a square, interconnecting, about a central court or patio. The name, *Su Casa*, was carved deep into the huge beam above the main gate, and the portals themselves were made of squared logs held together and hinged with straps of hand-hammered iron. The massive bastioned outer walls were three feet through and additionally strengthened by ramparts where the peons of the original owners could mount a withering defense. The old guard rooms, though crammed now with a dusty cobwebbed clutter of odds and ends, were still habitable at either side of the *puerta*, Rafe observed as he rode Bathsheba through the portals and came, not unnoticed, into the courtyard.

Here within the unpierced walls which had closed them off from the world outside, Ortega's family and retainers had lived a secluded life of their own. He could imagine dark faces curiously peering from the cell-like rooms lining the four sides of the patio and, almost, he could hear the pigs and goats foraging for scraps among the squawking flutter of scurrying hens that fled from beneath the skewbald's hoofs.

In the sun-laced shade of a giant pepper overhanging the stone-rimmed well, an old man sat in a wired-together rocker with a taffy haired girl, arrow straight, behind him. Between them and Rafe, caught frozen in midstride, Rafe saw the pulled-around darkening face of his brother.

'Evenin',' Rafe said, stepping out of the saddle, and saw the girl's hand come up and clutch at her throat.

'Who is it?' the old man called as Rafe came toward them; and Duke, pushing forward, said, 'I'll take care of this!'

One hand disappeared inside the green coat and Rafe, coldly grinning, not swerving by even the twitch of an eyebrow, walked right into him. Duke, cursing, fell back and then, with a kind of half-strangled scream, yanked the hand from his coat. Before he could bring the snub-nosed pistol into line Rafe's left hand closed like a vise around his wrist. Without visible effort Rafe dragged the arm up over Duke's head. Like a man with a possum up a tree he shook it, and the pistol flew into the well with a plop.

The old man, trying to get out of his chair, cried again, 'Who is it?' and Rafe, laughing into Duke's livid face, shoved him away. 'It's your son, Rafe,' he said, 'come back to take care of you.'

'Rafe?' the old man, brightening, got shakily up, the girl putting out her hands to help.

'He's not Rafe!' Duke snarled. 'Don't you remember? Rafe's *dead!*'

The light went out of old Bender's look. He stood there like a stricken oak, wide shoulders sagged, eyes dull, arms loose. 'Dead, you say? My son is dead ...' A shiver ran through the wasted frame, then the head tipped up. 'Neath tufted brows the eyes reached out like groping hands to find Rafe's shape and search his face and bewilderedly stretch from him to the girl. 'Luce—Luce,' he sighed, 'who is this man?'

Her eyes quit Duke, moving back to Rafe. 'I don't know,' she said, chin coming up. 'I never saw him before.'

'He looks to me,' growled Duke, 'like one of the bunch that's been liftin' our cows! We lost another big jag last night, Spangler says. I think—'

'Be still!' Bender cried. 'Let him speak for himself. I want to hear his voice.'

Rafe looked from the sullen hate on Duke's face to the cool unwinking stare of the girl. This wasn't the spindle-legged, big-eyed child who'd run clean to Beckston's Four Corners after him that day he'd gone to join up with Jeb Stuart. She'd shot up and filled out, become a real looker—if a man didn't peer too long or too deep.

He shook his head tiredly. 'What's to say when a man's own kin look him straight in the eye and don't know him from Adam—'

'You still claiming you're Rafe?'

'What difference does it make? Eleven years ain't a lifetime. I haven't changed that much.'

Bender said, 'Come over here, boy. Put your hand in mine and tell me you're Rafe—'

'Are you crazy?' Duke shouted. 'God damn it, Rafe's dead! We got a paper—'

'Where is this precious paper?' Rafe said.

Dog-eared and worn so thin along the creases you could pretty near look through them. Bender got it from his vest and, leaning against the well rim, tried with hands that shook to spread it out as Rafe stepped closer.

There didn't seem much point in reading it once his glance had taken in the official seal. It was bonafide enough; a number of women had got remarried, he'd heard, on the strength of papers like that. Give a man a kind of scalp-twitching feeling to come so sharp against proof he was dead. Made him wonder, by grab, if he wasn't better off to leave it!

Then he saw the covert exchange which passed between Duke and his sister; and he remembered how Joseph had been sold into Egypt. He thought, *They'll not get rid of me so free!* and said to his father, 'Seein's how I've come back, you can pitch that away.'

But Duke, rushing up, cried fierce through his teeth, 'No you don't—I'll take care of that!' and, before anyone realized what he was up to, grabbed the paper and defiantly crammed it into his pocket, backing hastily away.

Rafe, seeing his father's bewilderment, put a hand on his shoulder, the good hand, of course, because there wasn't very much he could do with the other. 'Never mind, suh. Let him have it,' he said. 'It's only a paper.

I'm right here beside you.'

The old man reached out and, milky stare peering blindly, suddenly stiffening when his touch came against that twisted claw. 'Boy, you lied. You're not Rafe—'

''Course he ain't!' Rafe's brother snarled. 'We tried to tell you! *Clabber 'im, Jess!*'

Something smoothly hard, something rigid as hate, came down like a house on the top of Rafe's head. His legs seemed to float right up off the ground.

CHAPTER SIX

He came out in black waves across teeth sharp as needles from the depths of incalculable time. And always, it seemed, to hover and bump as though trapped under glass just short of awareness.

This was something he seemed to do over and over with the pain splintering clean up into his shoulders in bursts of recurrent, almost intolerable, agony. More frequently then, with the pain subsiding, the invisible surface appeared to give just a little, to sway like thin ice when his weight came against it; he could imagine he saw light and, sometimes, a garble of sounds echoed fustily down through the shadowy cracks.

At last, in a lamplit room, he broke

through, owlishly blinking against the unaccustomed radiance. Eyes swimming into focus he beheld in startled wonder the peeled yeso-coated poles, a remembered halo of copper hair and, feeling bitterly put upon, clamped shut his eyes and dived incontinently back into the oblivion from which he had clawed.

Perhaps there was some good in it, but nothing was substantially altered next time he cautiously examined his whereabouts. He was still in Pike's house and Pike's filly was beside him. Also, like before, he was flat on his back in that dang female's bed!

It was a kind of situation no self-respecting Rebel could bring himself to countenance even for a minute if there had been any way around it. To be obligated once was cross enough for anyone. To find himself in their hands again—Rafe's eyes snapped shut with a shudder.

His mind cast back trying to think how he'd come here. He remembered Duke yelling, 'Clabber 'im, Jess!' and the world exploding like Harper's ferry, but the fog was too thick to fish anything else out.

Cracking open one eye he nervously took another squint. She was across the room now, sitting by the window with her head bent, sewing. You would never think to look at her she could be so dang deceitful, so demure she seemed, so quiet and sweet; but there'd been nothing sweet about the way she'd poked that sawed-off at him and Rafe wasn't about to forget it. Her old man, he reckoned, was probably gone to fetch the sheriff.

A sigh welled out of Rafe in spite of himself, and Bunny's head came up. 'Hi,' she said, her whole look disapproving. 'I suppose what has happened is the story of your life. In again, out again. When are you going to learn to take care of yourself?'

He was so piddlin' weak he couldn't seem, even, to work up a decent outrage. She put her sewing aside and, not waiting for an answer, got up and went off.

Through the door she'd left open he could hear her bustling around in the kitchen. Pretty soon the mouth-priming aroma of chicken made him think he'd pass out before she got the stuff to him.

When she finally came with a bowl of water the gird had been rinsed in he was too whipped to protest; so weak, by grab, he couldn't even get his hands from under the covers. He had to lay there and let her spoon it into him.

Next time he came around it was Pike who sat watching. Pike looking thoughtful, said, 'How you feel? Up to taking more nourishment?'

Rafe had been determined to have it out with the feller, but the needs of the body appeared suddenly more important than making clear where he stood on the subject of Yankees. Sourly scowling, he nodded.

'Bunny—' Pike called, 'fetch in the rest of that broth and a soft boiled egg. Bring a handful of crackers. And a mug of weak tea.'

Rafe said, glowering, 'You got to kill me by inches?'

'You'll live through it,' Pike chuckled, 'if we can keep down the complications. What'd you do to that hand?'

'Hand...? Oh! Horse rolled on it. In the war. I was—'

'You told me about that. I'm talking about the one you were using when you tore out of here.'

Seeing Rafe's puzzlement Pike reached out and pulled down the covers. Rafe was dumbfounded. Both hands were bandaged clean to the elbows. He couldn't move either one; 'Looked to me,' Pike said, 'like someone took a club to you. That left hand of yours was in bad shape: Thought I might just as well work on both of them while I was at it.'

Rafe stared at the wrappings, trying to understand what had happened, but too shocked, too confused, to get really hold of anything beyond the appalling notion that this gross tub of lard had used him for a guinea pig. And that no matter if he wound up maimed for life—He said, feeling sick,

'Am I going to be able to use 'em?'

Pike regarded him across steepled fingers. 'Little early yet to say.' He stared a while longer, settling back with a chuckle. 'At least you won't be much worse off than I found you.'

'And where was that,' Rafe finally said.

'In the Dunes. There was quite a gale coming up. It's a wonder those shifting hills hadn't buried you.'

Rafe reckoned that was probably what they had put him out there for.

'What happened to the mare?'

'Some ranch hand found her halfway to Willcox,' Pike said with his look playing over Rafe's face. 'She was pretty sore footed, didn't have a shoe on her. Sheriff went over and picked her up couple of weeks ago.'

Presently Rafe, uncommonly meek, said, 'About how far from where you found me was she?'

'About forty miles.'

A kind of quiet set in through which, peculiarly, both men stared. Then Pike with a wheezing groan got up. 'Somebody worked you over plenty. Sheriff's going to want to know about that. Probably be by to pick up your statement. You damn well better be around when he gets here.'

It was hard for Rafe to realize that more than two weeks had dropped right out of his life while he'd been flat on his back and out of his head. And he was sorely confused. It wasn't like a Yankee to be so diligent on behalf of an obviously down-and-out Rebel.

Bunny came in with the slop that Pike had called for, fluffed up his pillows, and proceeded to feed him. This she did with a determined cheer, chattering on, apparently paying no mind to Rafe's black scowls and rather niggardly replies.

He didn't even bother to make out like he was listening; he was too upset, too taken up with his worries.

She broke off, sat back, looking reproachful, a little indignant. 'If you think this is fun for me—' she began, then with color coming into her cheeks let it go. 'Tomorrow we're going to get you out of that bed.' She pushed the last spoonful of broth-clammy crackers into his mouth. 'Daddy says I'm not to stop you, that if you want to climb through that window again you'll not be hurting anyone but yourself. I do hope though,' she said, regarding him slanchways, 'that this time you'll at least *think* before you leap.'

She had his attention now, all right. Every last scalp-prickling bit of it. 'You—' he licked dry lips, 'you mean I'm free to go? That I can walk right outa here any time I want?'

She stared back at him unreadably. At last, with a sniff, she gathered up her eating tools, got out of her chair. But at the door she looked back; almost, he thought, with a kind of reluctant pity. 'I've told you all I can,' she said.

CHAPTER SEVEN

Rafe felt the cold prickles digging into his belly. So that was their game! The old *ley del fuego*—law of escape. It was plain enough now why the sheriff in all this while hadn't got around to visiting him. They didn't want to hear no stories from him. They was too damn scared what he'd say might embarrass them!

And maybe they wasn't too far wrong at that. Their tin-badge sure knew which pocket the bulk of his living come out of. He wouldn't want to cross that penny-pinching banker; and the whole shebang likely knew by now Pike's patient wasn't nothing but another whipped Rebel. Rattle him, get the bastard's wind up, and then when he hopped through that window nail him! Who was going to kick up a stink over what the law did to any cut-and-run sesech saddle bum?

He could feel the sweat coming through his skin. Some goddamn Rebel was always getting himself killed. Nothing new about that. If it hadn't been for the girl—but this was no time to be thinking about her! It was *him* they was figuring to shut up. That was plain enough. This time they'd do it proper!

It didn't make no difference in Rafe's tangled thinking that all of his assumptions might not actually be true. He'd had nothing but trouble since he'd come into this country and he was, by grab, getting plenty fed up.

True to Bunny's promise they got him out of her bed the very next day; gave him steak, too, all he could cram into him. They sure was in a sweat to get him up and about and off on his own again. Pike, evidently, had been told to get rid of him.

It wasn't too easy to understand when you came right down to it. That banker, Chilton, cracked the whip around here—he'd stood Dahl off, no doubt about that. And Rafe was Chilton's man, on the surface anyway. Or had the highbinder washed his hands of Rafe after learning he was back in Pike's care, busted up? Had he learned the whole story of what had happened out yonder, or was it just Rafe's failure which had brought this shift in plans?

Nothing Rafe hit on seemed to make much sense. But with Bunny's cryptic words still rattling around through the corridors of his mind he was in no hurry to get back into circulation. A third week passed almost before he was aware of it. Except that his flippers were still swathed in bandages he was beginning to feel more his natural self.

Pike helped him into his clothes every morning. Bunny fed and shaved him, gave him the run of the entire house. Her father washed him. The girl helped him on and off with his boots. He managed to hold back the calls of nature until Pike was around and then, some days later, the old red nosed boozer took off the wraps to have a squint at his handiwork.

Rafe was most nigh scairt to look himself. He peered at the flesh serving Pike for a face but might's well have quartered a rock, he thought, for all the good he got out of it. Then he saw Pike's eyes and very near quit breathing.

When he got hold of his courage, he said pretty bitter, 'You got to take off both of 'em?'

'Eh? No, no, nothing like that,' Pike said, covering up with a heartiness obviously as spurious as a three-dollar bill. 'Turned out a deal better than we'd any right to hope for. Try moving those fingers. Here, let me massage them.'

Rafe still wouldn't look, but there was plenty of feeling. He damn near climbed right out of the chair. Through clamp-shut eyes he snarled, 'You tryin' to break 'em!'

'Take it easy,' Doc said. 'This is very encouraging.' He went on with whatever it was he was doing. 'Feel like pins and needles going through them?'

It took all Rafe's breath to keep from yelling. When he reluctantly slatted one eye to take a peek Doc, settled back, had let go and was smiling. 'You're going to have to get used to it, Bender. A lot of tissue was crushed. It's impaired the circulation. You're going to have to exercise—'

'How'd you know my name was Bender?'

'Isn't that what you told Bunny?'

Rafe didn't like Pike's stare. It put him in mind of the way the girl had looked when he had told her his name, when he'd been answering all them questions. It came over him now she'd hooked him up straightaway with the horse spread out at the Ortega place; and he wondered if Chilton had made this connection—if, indeed, it hadn't been the basis of his interest, of that job he'd dug straight out of the barrel.

He demanded, glowering, 'Who else knows about it?'

Pike fished a bottle out of his pocket. When Rafe testily looked his disgust and contempt, Bunny's father, shrugging, put about ten swallows hurriedly down his own hatch. Smacking his lips with a satisfied sigh the old gaffer said, 'Whole town, probably. But I will tell you this—they never got it from us. The relationship between a patient and his doctor—wild horses couldn't have dragged it out of us! And,' he declared, leaning precariously nearer, 'I don't believe

Chilton knew about it when he hired you.'

Though Rafe couldn't follow the convolutions of Pike's reasoning, and didn't for a moment put any stock in his protestations, the Doc's final statement rang a bell deep inside him.

'How do you figure that?' he said.

'He's up to his ears in that place, been itching to take it over,' Pike urged, 'ever since he fixed up those papers for Bender. Spangler's the only thing that's stood in his way. You think he'd have steered you into the deal if he'd had any notion your name was the same?'

'Maybe not,' Rafe growled, 'but if Spangler is takin' all the profits outa the spread I can't see how he's hurtin' Chilton any. I would say he's playin' right into Chilton's—'

'That's because,' Pike said darkly, 'you don't—' and chopped off his talk as Bunny came wide-eyed into the room.

'Oh!' she cried, suddenly smiling, 'you've got the bandages off. I'm so glad!' She looked at her father. 'He'll be all right now, won't he? He'll be able to use them?'

Pike with his mouth puckered up looked undecided. He finally said, 'I don't really know. If he keeps working them, puts in the time and the patience it will take, I'd say that right hand will maybe come out pretty good; but the left—They didn't leave much to work with. He'll get some use out of those fingers, but the first and third—I really ought to open.'

'Not on your tintype!' Rafe snarled, glowering, and lividly thrust both hands behind him. Bunny looked shocked. Almost reproachfully, she said, 'If Daddy thinks—'

'By grannies,' Rafe shouted, backing hastily away, 'I don't care *what* he thinks! They're my hands, dammit! And they've had all the monkeyin' I'm goin' to stand for, you hear?' he yelled, bowing up like a cornered cat.

Bunny, appearing dismayed and bewildered, said, 'But Daddy—'

'Never mind! I'll make out, don't you worry! Send me your bill. I'll pay it when I can, but don't either one of you come any nearer. I'm gittin' outa here an' nobody, believe me, better get in my way!'

'But you *can't!*' Bunny wailed. 'Don't you know that's what they *want?*' She whipped around. 'Daddy, tell him!'

Pike, sighing mightily, steepled his fingers. 'I'm afraid your life wouldn't be worth a plugged nickel if they were to catch you out of this house right now.'

Rafe, bristling with distrust, was half convinced in spite of himself. '"They"? What "they"? You talkin' about that squirrel-faced banker an' his bought-an-paid-for sheriff?'

Pike's eyes kind of goggled. His jaw flopped down like a blacksmith's apron. 'Great Scott!' he exclaimed, sounding pretty upset. Peering nervously around, and with all his chins quivering, he cautiously lowered his elephant-like behind. With a considerable expulsion of grunts and wheezes he eventually got it settled in the chair. 'Young man,' he said, 'the subject of your remarks is not one to be taken lightly.' His simmering stare swiveled around to his daughter. 'Show him, Bunny.'

'Come along,' she bade with her own glance averted, and Rafe followed her out into a room that faced the street. He trailed her over to the window. Being careful not to disturb the curtain she said, 'Take a look at that.'

Straight off Rafe didn't see a thing but the scenery. Then the wink of metal drew his narrowing stare to a scrub oak thicket a couple of hundred feet away. Barely discernible through the foliage was the shape of a squatting man.

Bunny touched his arm and they returned to the bedroom where she stopped beside her father. Following her eyes Rafe went again to look out. Another man was waiting in the rocks beyond the shed from which, the first time he'd quit this place, he'd got Bathsheba. 'Well?' he said, staring hard at Pike. 'What's about it?'

'If this were Chilton's doing,' Bunny's father said, 'they'd not need to be under cover.'

But Rafe wasn't ready to holler calf rope yet. 'Maybe,' he said, 'his tin-badge had other fish to fry.'

'You can't have it both ways,' Bunny exclaimed indignantly. 'If the sheriff was hand-in-glove with Mr. Chilton, and it was Mr. Chilton's intention to put you out of business, you'd be in jail right now. To be made a public example of!'

'Maybe it didn't suit—'

'Boy,' Pike said, 'I've heard enough of that nonsense. The facts speak for themselves. That pair you've just looked at are a couple of Spangler hardcases, and they're obviously out there to make sure you stay put.'

Not even Rafe's hardshell prejudice could stand up against that. But he wasn't about to step down without a struggle. 'Then why don't this wonderful Dry Bottom badge-toter make 'em clear out or shove 'em in the clink?'

Bunny, looking flustered, clouded up to say resentfully, 'Nobody with a lick of sense would go out of his way to tangle with Spangler.'

'Well, isn't that just fine!' Rafe scowled. 'What's a feller have to do to get protection around here?'

'Mostly, around here,' Pike said, staring

back at him, 'a crock is expected to stand on its own bottom.'

CHAPTER EIGHT

Say what you will, that following week was the longest Rafe Bender had ever put in at anything. Whenever he looked Spangler's gunnies was out there. Maybe not the same pair all this miserable while, but there wasn't an hour there wasn't somebody at it, watching and waiting like a couple of damned toads. More than once he was almost tempted to step out, so fierce was the pressure, so frustrating the fury being piled up inside him.

He became hard to live with as Bunny had frankly said one day. But he was not too filled with his persecutions to forget the exercises Pike had prescribed. Hour after hour he worked his fingers, kneeding them, stretching them, flexing and bending them while the hate coursed through him like a heavy tide. He could feed himself now, could dress and shave himself too, do pretty near anything else but get out of there.

One thing he had made up his mind about: hereafter he was going to look out for himself, and the devil take the rest of them. There was no good trying to be a turn-your-cheek Christian in a land overrun by throat-slitting Philistines. From here on out he would be playing for Rafe Bender!

He could put together a smoke with his hands now, but the left, as Pike feared, healed up considerable short of maximum efficiency. Oh, it would pick up things and, after a fashion, manage to keep hold of them, but those first and third fingers didn't close the way they ought to. They tracked; that was about all you could say for them. He'd had to learn all over again to work at old skills that right hand had forgotten. Lifting and squeezing he kept both of them busy while he built back his strength and nursed his black fury.

Saturday the sheriff came, a washed-out, handlebarred, frame-shrunk old has-been whose rheumy eyes appeared frequently to seek but never quite meet the pair staring back at him. Dropping his hat on the floor he took the proffered chair, heeled it back against the wall and said, 'You've had a time, I guess.'

Rafe considered that self-evident. Pike wasn't home and Bunny, after introducing the badge-toter as Ed Sparks, had gone back to the kitchen, leaving them alone.

'Mebbe,' Sparks said now, 'you better tell me about it.'

'What's there to tell? Somebody beat the livin' daylights out of me, packed me off and left me out in them dunes to get blowed over with sand an' buried.'

'You don't *know* that, do you? I understood, when the coroner found you, you was ravin' like a loony, plumb out of your head.'

'What's that got to do with the price of apples?'

'How would you know, then, how you got out there?'

'If I'd set out by shank's mare I would know it!'

The sheriff stared at Rafe's run-over boots and shifted his chaw to the other side of his face. 'You say somebody beat you. Care to put a name to him?'

'I don't know who it was.'

'Ain't that a mite strange? I think if somebody'd handled me the way you been—'

'I was talkin',' Rafe growled, 'when somebody bent a gun over my noggin. I didn't see him—Hell, you don't think I'm nump enough to take that *deliberate!*'

'Well ... where was this? Who was you talkin' to?'

'I ain't askin' your help.'

'I'll thank you to recollect I'm sheriff of these parts. I've got a right to expect you to answer my questions, boy.'

'Go right ahead an' expect if you want to.'

Sparks' cheeks flushed a little, but his eyes

juned away. 'Understand you fought for the Rebs durin' the war.' He stopped to let Rafe consider the fact. 'A man gets farther an' a whole heap faster—'

'If you got a point, make it.'

'I want to know where that gun was bent over your head. I want to know who done it an' who you was talkin' to.' He said, suddenly scowling, 'I want to know all about it.'

Rafe grinned.

'All right,' Sparks spat, 'be a pig-headed fool, but don't come cryin' to me if you're killed!' He scooped up his hat and got onto his feet. 'I don't want no trouble breakin' out account of you.'

'A man's got a right to defend—'

'A Rebel's got no rights at all around here. If your health's become a problem I suggest you take it to where the climate's more salubrious. You understand that?'

Rafe bristled up, eyes bright as bottle glass. 'Don't bang your threats against me, you dang boot licker!' Looking about to throw a fit he started for the man. Sparks scrinched away. Squirming along the wall the sheriff made it to the door and scuttled off down the hall like he had ants in his pants.

Rafe, glowering after him, slammed the door so violently that, off out of sight, something fell with a clatter. Still muttering, fierce scowling, he threw open the window to blow the place out.

But there wasn't so much as a breath of air stirring. All the open window did was let in more heat, and with a snarl of disgust Rafe picked up his shell belt and buckled it around him, looking sure enough about as rile as a man could get.

He wished now he'd asked what Sparks proposed to do about the pair outside that was keeping him bottled up in this place—not that he was like to have done anything anyway. At least it would have given Rafe a chance to work off some of his spleen. Still thinking about it, he hauled open the door and went prowling for Bunny.

She was still in the kitchen, flour on her arms and dough on the bread board. She looked around with a smile that tried hard to stay as she took in, sobering, the signs of Rafe's mood. She said, 'It won't be forever, if that's any consolation. Why don't you go sit on the porch and cool off?'

He said, in self-pity, 'You tryin' to get me a harp?'

'I don't think those fellows will do anything so long as they believe you're not trying to duck out.'

'Well, thanks,' Rafe said thinly. 'Sure pleasures my thinkin' a heap to hear that!'

She made a little face. Then she sighed, prodding her dough. 'Most of the boys I knew back home, if they'd been cooped up like this with a girl, would have better things to do with their time than moping around, fretting and stewing, the way you've been ever since you've been up.'

Rafe, stopped short, went still as a fence post, looking at her as though she's sprouted two heads.

'They'd know a girl likes to be noticed. Probably most of them,' she said, going on with her work, 'would have first of all figured on improving their acquaintance.'

Rafe's mouth dropped open. His cheeks fired up. His eyes bugged out like two knobs on a stick.

She slanched him a look as she was rolling out her dough. 'I guess those tales I've heard of Southern gallantry—'

Rafe, anyway, had heard more than enough. He got out of that kitchen like the heel flies was after him.

'Lordy!' he breathed, propping a chair against his door, eyes big as slop buckets. He dragged a sleeve across his face, sagged into the chair, looking about as limp as a bundle of dish rags. Talk about your Delilahs! He'd encountered some pretty designing females in some of the places he'd been since the War but never, by grab, any girl bold as her!

He got onto his feet with his clothes sticking to him, too upset to think straight, too indignant to sit still; and yet, someway, filled with a strange and delicious excitement. He realized this was her wiles tightening round him. There was no defense against a scheming woman—or, he thought, suddenly colder than frog legs, a woman scorned! And it was no danged help for him to stand here shaking. He'd better dig for the tules—*andale pronto!*

This was the straw he fastened to in his perturbation, completely forgetting the gunhawks outside. He found his hat and chin-strapped it to him, was taking a last nervous look around when remembrance of Spangler's henchmen hit, pretty near taking the legs out from under him. With both fists gripped to the sash he stopped.

'Lord God a'mighty!' he gasped, backing off. He saw his goggling stare dreadfully reflected in the wavery hand-rolled lights of the window. He gulped for wind, swallowing like he'd got a bone in his throat, shuddery sort of, all his thoughts upside down.

He made a real effort to pull himself together, desperately trying to drive back the unnerving vision of Spangler's hardfaced pistoleros. If they were still out there, and their job was to get him, you could dang well bet they'd make their try—but you couldn't tell what a fool female might do—probably whatever popped into her head; and just the bare thought was more than Rafe could put up with. He grabbed a quick breath and made a dash for the door.

And the worst of it was he might have got clean away with it. But just as his best hand went out to yank it open, Bunny's voice called. Letting go of the knob Rafe jerked half around, flopping like a fish with a hook through its gills.

She was in the kitchen doorway with her blue rounded eyes looking big almost as teacups. One flour-daubed hand was against her throat and Rafe, for the life of him, couldn't say a thing. Filled with guilt and consternation he reckoned she'd seen right enough what he was up to. It gave him a turn the way she looked, so forlorn and defeated, so someway wistful.

'Rafe!'

You'd of swore her cry came straight from the heart. A man just plain couldn't help being affected; Rafe stood with bowed shoulders, itchy with embarrassment, feeling—dad drat it—like a damn caught Judas!

By girding himself, looking off past her, he could ignore the unexpected brimming of tears, but he had no shield against the words that came tumbling so pitifully out of her. 'You,' she gulped, 'were figuring to go without ever a word?'

He stared at the floor, trying to shut out the sound, seeming about as low down as a growed man could get. She honestly had him, coming and going; but, woman fashion, couldn't leave it there. She had to rub his nose in it.

'After all we've been to each other.' She sighed. 'Oh, Rafe—how *could* you!'

Since they hadn't been anything at all to each other, this struck a jarring off-key chord in a man who, though groggy, was still on his feet. It was just like pumping new blood through his veins. Time she came, groping, arms out and reaching toward him, Rafe had got off the hook and was going through the door.

CHAPTER NINE

The man out front must have been plumb asleep. Rafe, hunting Bathsheba, got clean around the house and halfway to the shed before he got loose enough of the spell she'd put on him to remember Spangler's gunnies. With a startled yelp he plunged against the door, only to find it re-enforced with a padlock!

Rafe didn't waste any time shouting curses. He dragged out his pistol and banged the butt against the thing, again and again until the lock flopped open.

Bathsheba, pawing, bobbed her head and whinnied. Rafe found the blanket and got his saddle on her. The bridle and bit he had missed before were hung with his spurs from a peg on the wall and, though he shivered with impatience, he got them too, dug his boot in the stirrup and went on up.

The mare danced with excitement as he kneed her around. Rafe, truth to tell, was pretty excited himself, expecting any moment to hear the yells go up. Quick as he got her facing the door he brought the reins down hard. She went through like a thrown rock, grunting and squealing, breaking wind at every jump.

He heard the first shot whimper *cousin*, slicing the air about an inch from his jaw. But he held his fire, scrinching flat out along the mare's extended neck, not daring now to swerve her; and this way, her shod hoofs pounding up a storm, they sailed into the open, straight as an arrow for the front of Pike's house.

That whippoorwill back in the rocks was really talking but Rafe, though he had his Colt in his hand, was a deal more worried about the one out front who'd be having a broadside target soon as they cleared this end of the house.

And now they were doing it. Now Rafe could see the front porch, and beyond it the dust churning struggle of two limb-tangled shapes furiously locked in grim combat. Bunny's red hair was flying around every whichway, and even as Rafe looked Spangler's man flung her off and snapped up his rifle. Rafe squeezed the trigger, missed, and squeezed off another. The rifleman, clutching his belly, teetered back on both boot heels and went down like a sack.

Now Rafe was into the brush, tearing noisily through it, covering his head against the slap of the branches; not aiming this time to go into the town, not a thought in his head at the moment but escape. The surviving Spangler hand was bound to take after him, and all Rafe had for defense was his six-shooter, not very substantial deterrent against hardcase armed with a rifle. Rafe was counting heavy on the mare's long rest to open up a lead to where he'd have some chance of losing the feller.

Then a fresh thought hit him. Maybe that bird from the rocks wasn't following. He must know this country a heap better than Rafe, could probably guess within a matter of yards where his quarry would emerge and even now be racing to get there ahead of him.

Rafe pulled up to listen. Beyond the restless stomp and panting of the mare he couldn't hear much of anything. He'd been intending, soon as he got clear of this growth, to get into the hills and maybe hole up until he could get some line on how things were shaping. This still looked a pretty solid idea, but he wouldn't get far charging into no rifle. Town, for the moment, might prove healthiest after all.

He reined the mare left and, holding her to a walk, tried to sift a few facts from the tangle of his confusion. It was not too surprising his thoughts went to the girl. From what little he actually knew, or had observed, there was very little evidence to nourish the suspicions he'd embraced that Bunny and her father were purely out to do him dirt. And yet, that business back at the house lacked considerable of offering any real proof they weren't. Her struggle with that rifle packer could have had some entirely different significance, nothing to do with him at all. At very best, he decided, the most you could get out of it was that she hadn't wanted Rafe killed.

It would pay a man to be almighty cautious in assessing any actions of a girl bold as Bunny. Rafe wasn't too depressed about the gun-waver he had shot. He would like to have done as much for that other one.

He replaced the spent loads and observed that his cover was about to play out. Through the branches ahead he could see the town's buildings. Considering the risks of shewing himself, he was forced to the rather reluctant conclusion that the safest place for Rafe Bender right now in Dry Bottom would be Alph Chilton's bank.

He could see its brick shape a couple of hundred yards off, and pulled up again in the last of the brush for a prolonged, intent and pretty scowling appraisal. The backs of buildings seldom offer, with their rubbish of rusting tins, broken crates and flapping paper, a particularly inspiring sight, but Rafe guessed he should be thankful to be looking at their behinds. There were worse things a man could stare at. Back lots, anyway, didn't get much traffic. With reasonable luck a man ought to be able to get from here to there in one piece, if he was careful.

It bothered him, though, not to see any sign of that feller from the rocks, the shot guy's pard. If the bleach-eyed son had took out to nail him, it was natural to think that when Rafe hadn't shown where he had been looked for, the feller would have come on into town to do his hunting. Rafe would have done it.

Behind his screen of branches Rafe swung down to rest and stretch the kinks from his legs while he waited to see if Spangler's gunhawk would show. After about ten minutes of standing around, the skewbald mare began to paw with impatience, bumping Rafe's shoulder with vigorous pokes of her head. 'Dang it, quit!' Rafe growled, batting her away with his hat.

He got out the makings, rolled up a smoke and, with his eyes going narrow, suddenly pitched it away. He dropped the reins to the ground; then, thinking better of this, tied them to a sapling stout enough to keep her anchored, it being in his mind Spangler's gunnie may have gone back to pick up his tracks.

It was a sensible assumption and Rafe, proceeding to act on it, again drew his pistol, creeping back along his trail with all the stealth of a crouching puma. He knew, by grannies, he had *better* be careful, or be ready, like fiddlers, to wind up in hell. In country like this there wasn't much leg room betwixt the quick and them that hadn't been quite quick enough.

And so it was that, presently, Rafe's aching vigilance fastened onto an impression of approaching movement. It wasn't scarcely more than a hunch when he got into it, not much easier to be gauged than the footfalls of a gopher, the merest whisperings of sound. But it snapped up his hackles.

With his eyes stabbing about he scanned the surroundings and his chances. Impatiently shaking his head he moved on, hunting terrain better suited to his needs, knowing from experience with Stuart during the war that a fracas fought on ground of one's choosing was a squabble more likely to fetch a man out on top.

Rafe had had more than his fill of killing, but even a kid in three-cornered pants would have savvy enough to know this whippoorwill had to be stopped. There was no two ways around that!

He came over a rise and found what he wanted, a tiny twenty-foot clearing with a rock to one side of it big enough to easily hide a waiting man. The sounds were plain enough now, snap and crackle of branches, a shod hoof scraping stone. Rafe, eyes slitted, pistol tight in his fist—the one Pike had fixed for him, backed into the clearing, hurried over to the rock, moving clear on around it and, careful now to conceal his flight, circled back to the rise and dropped, breathing hard, behind it.

That right hand wasn't right even yet. It still had twinges and there was times when the muscles didn't work like they had ought to but he had proved back at Pike's it was good enough to shoot with. Not that he was anxious to do any shooting; this close to town he hated even to think of it. But if he had learned one thing on that trip to the Benders he had learned how much help he could count on from them.

Now the sounds were close enough to sort out. It was plain the feller had got out of his saddle; you could hear the scrape and scuff of his boots in between the sharper footfalls of his horse; probably leading the critter. It was easy to picture them that way, the man crouched over, eyes batting around, as he unraveled Rafe's sign.

If this was Spangler's gun fighter he wouldn't be used to this kind of thing, likely making hard work of it, getting madder with every stride. But, account of his trade, he'd have his eyes peeled too, which could account for the time it had taken him to get here.

Rafe, ears stretched, held his breath in cold suspense, knowing the feller must be pretty near up to where those tracks he'd just made took off toward the rock. Would the bastard notice? Would suspicion bite into him? Would he come straight on, paying no attention to the overlay of boot marks?

All sound suddenly quit. By this it was obvious the man had spotted something. The horse shook its head, Rafe heard its bit chains, the crop of its teeth going through green stems. Feller'd probably left it. Rafe dared not wait any longer.

Pistol lifting he raised up off the ground, coming onto his knees, enabled by this to see a part of the clearing, the man's head and shoulders. About three strides from his horse and faced half away the feller, crouched above a rifle, had his stare fixed on the rock.

'Lookin' for me?' Rafe called, and you could see the shock of it hit the guy, and then he was whirling, Rafe crying fiercely, 'Drop it, you fool!'

The man was mightily tempted. It was in

the brightness of that spinning look, in the whiteness of his knuckles. But in the end he let the carbine go.

Rafe licked his lips. 'An' now the belt.'

The guy had to make his fight all over, but the best chance was gone. He unbuckled the belt with a bitter sigh, the weight of it slithering down his legs.

Rafe said thinly, 'Hike over to that rock. An' be careful, mister. I'll be right behind you.'

The feller uncorked some pretty foul language but in the end, still grumbling, strode off in the direction indicated. Rafe was right on his heels. Just before they arrived at the rock the barrel of Rafe's six-shooter flashed up and came down across the top of the man's head. He staggered, trying to turn, and then, eyes hating, went down in a heap.

In a matter of moments Rafe had him gagged and sufficiently trussed that it should be some while before he'd be in a position to discuss what had happened. Rafe went back to the man's mount, dumped off the saddle, slipped the headstall and, with a whack of his hat, sent the horse larruping south. The animal might not go far, but he would sure as hell take some hunting.

Now that he had this weight off his back there was no urgent reason for Rafe going into Dry Bottom. He could head for the hills above the Ortega Grant, and this he was considerably minded to do, but to get into that country there were plenty of desert miles to be covered. Nobody who had his head on straight would figure on thumbing his nose at no desert, and you wouldn't get far carrying water in your hat.

Looked like he was going to have to go into town anyway. And if he took that much risk he might as well go whole hog and *habla* with Chilton. He sure didn't put no trust in that feller, but the banker appeared to call the tunes around here. A man would get farther under his umbrella than he could mucking around as a masterless Rebel. Rafe guessed he'd better find out where he stood.

Hurrying back to Bathsheba he climbed into the saddle and kneed the mare out into the open. He felt about as conspicuous traveling those back lots as a goldfish swimming through a dish of tea. There might be others of Spangler's crowd in this town, and there was no doubt at all how Jack Dahl felt with the wreck of his place probably still unpaid for. But Rafe wasn't going back across that desert without water, not with Duke's whole crew maybe out there waiting for him.

He couldn't see, as he drew nearer, that he'd attracted any attention. If there was people on the street he guessed they was mostly under the wooden awnings; there sure didn't seem to be much going on. Coming up in back of the bank he took another long look and reluctantly got down, and stood another couple of minutes before he turned loose of the reins. Rubbing his fists, nervously flexing his fingers, he walked around to the front and gingerly stepped in.

The same moth-eaten moose heads stared down from the walls and the same dusty eagle was roosting over the door to the big man's private cubbyhole. Then he saw Jack Dahl with his face black as thunder coming out of the banker's suddenly flung-open door. But the man stomped past without a second look. He was sure grinding his molars. Rafe, bringing his head around, went on in.

Ed Sparks with a wheatstraw clamped in his jaw stood beside the banker's desk, hat in hand, his look as devoid of expression as a gambler crouched over an ace-full on queens.

The banker said, 'Well, so you've finally come round,' and drummed fat fingers while he considered Rafe uncharitably. Then he said, very dry, 'That'll be all for now, Ed.'

Sparks put on his hat and departed.

'Close the door,' Chilton said, and after Rafe heeled it shut, 'How'd you get past Spangler's snipers?'

Rafe told him. Then, thumbs hooked over shell belt, he grumbled, 'Didn't reckon you'd have any more time to waste on a feller that stacked up no better than I did.'

'That bastard's still in the saddle.'

Rafe stared, finally nodding.

'What happened?'

'Well, I went out there,' Rafe said, wondering how much the old skinflint knew. 'Reckon you figured, on account of the name, it would be apple pie with brown sugar on it.' He snorted. 'We never got down to the huggin' an' kissin'. Not even the girl would give in I was Rafe. Whilst I was augerin' with Duke an' her father some warthog snuck up an' bent a gun over my head. When I come to I was back here in town. Guess that's about the size of it.'

The banker reached a cheroot from a box, ran a tongue over its dryness, poked it into his face and fired up. Rolling the weed across crockery teeth while he continued to stare, he said through the smoke, 'And what name were you born with?'

'The same. Rafe Bender.'

The banker's hard eyes crawled over him like beetles. His cheroot lobbed out smoke. 'Can you make it stick?'

'I'm goin' to sure as hell try!'

CHAPTER TEN

'Well, it figures,' Chilton sighed after another intent look. 'What about your hands? This ain't going to be duck soup.'

'I ain't goin' to be caught like that again, neither.' Rafe scowled, impatient with so much jawing. 'Am I still on the payroll or ain't I?'

Chilton puffed some more, finally pitched his stogie into a spittoon. 'I don't figure to pour good money after bad—'

'Hell's fire!' Rafe snarled. 'You ain't put a cent in my pockets up to now!' Looking rabid, he leaned over Chilton's desk. 'I got to eat, too! I been pretty hard used goin' after your chestnuts—'

'All right,' the banker said in a considerably milder tone, 'we can do business. But make sure you remember I can't afford to have my name linked with failures. Next time you come out the bottom side of the deck you better spread your wings and keep right on going.'

Though he fumed inside, Rafe was unable to find a match for such words. In any deal with this kind of whistleberry, a man was outvoted from scratch. Just the same, determined to have the last say, he growled. 'I'll need a canteen, a good high-powered rifle—better get me a tellyscope, too, while you're at it. An' a couple of weeks' grub, an' a pack horse to tote 'em. An' if you don't want that guy I tied up bargin' in, better send someone out for this stuff in a hurry.'

They glowered at each other. But Rafe, in this matter, was top dog, and both knew it. Looking riled enough to chew up bar iron, Chilton called in one of his clerks and gave instructions. 'An' fetch 'im around to the back,' Rafe said, boldly helping himself from Chilton's box of cheroots.

Filling the place with its stink he struck a lucifer, igniting the weed he had in his mouth while he stuffed a half dozen others into his shirt. The banker kept still, but there was in his look the definite promise of hard times to come. He was the kind who forgot nothing, who demanded six bits for every dime he put out. There would be a hereafter. Rafe never doubted that.

But it did him good to see the man writhe. He said, spewing smoke like a half-clogged chimney, 'Let's get down to brass tacks. How did old Bender git his hooks on that ranch?'

Chilton finally said, 'He won it at cards.'

When Rafe's eyebrows went up the banker grudgingly said, 'Don Luis was a plunger, one of those all-or-nothing fools. Vain, flamboyant, proud as a peacock. And, like all of his tribe, couldn't see beyond his nose. He couldn't imagine a time,' Chilton said with contempt, 'when Ortegas wouldn't be right next to God, when all they had known would leak away through his fingers. Don Luis the Magnificent! He hadn't the sense to pound sand down a rat hole!'

'But the ranch?' Rafe prodded.

'Bender had just come into the country. Had lost this fellow Rafe in the War and had just lost his wife; didn't seem to care whether school kept or not. He was at the bar in Jack Dahl's place when Ortega came in, the crowd opening up to let him through. Wanted Bender's horses so bad he could taste them. You wouldn' have known he was drunk, I'll say that for him. He could really put it away.'

'You was there?'

Chilton nodded. 'Bender was pretty well tanked himself, but not so far gone he'd sell stock he had driven all the way from the Ozarks. Don Luis kept raising the price. Bender kept stubbornly shaking his head. All this while they kept pouring it down. Finally Ortega offered to put up his ranch on the turn of a card—the land and the buildings against Bender's horses.

'I'd been pointed out to Bender; matter of fact, Dahl had made us acquainted. Knowing I was a banker Bender asked what I thought, and I told him I'd put up thirty thousand against it. Well, Bender won; next day he came along and asked for the money.'

'An' just like that you put it up.'

Chilton's stare eyed him coldly. 'Finally, yes. But not in one chunk. First time he got half; twice, later, for improvements, he picked up the rest.'

'What improvements?'

'The deal,' Chilton said, 'was between him and me.' A grin twitched his lips and he got out of his chair. 'Your outfit's ready.' And, before Rafe hardly knew what was happening, he was outside the bank. 'All you need worry about,' Chilton said just before he shut and bolted the door, 'is getting rid of Spangler. Don't come back till you've done it.'

Two hours later, deep into the desert, Rafe pulled up for the sixth time to rest his horses and take a long scowl at the country behind. He'd got away from town without any trouble. It had been blowing pretty fierce, and the scud of grit had evidently chased most of the loafers inside. He'd run out of the wind before he'd come three miles, and this was when he'd taken his first look. Nothing showed then, or at any of his later stops, nor could he see any sign of movement now.

The sun was a ball of blazing fire. Distant mountains were half lost in the haze. The white glare was beginning to cook his face and he frustratedly scrubbed it with the back of a hand. The landscape curled and writhed in the heat, and in all those miles of barren waste the only motion to be glimpsed was the twist of a dust devil blowing itself apart.

Rafe was not reassured. The emptiness only increased his uneasiness, deepening his sense of isolation. Though he couldn't find a thing, he was convinced he was being followed; it had been gnawing at him for more than an hour. Now he saw a chance to make sure.

Up ahead about a mile was a long dark ridge, a volcanic spine blown clean of sand and lifting perhaps a dozen feet above the floor. This would give a man cover, and if he cut west behind it and observed proper caution he should be able to come back on his tracks in a circle. It would mean being stuck out here for the night. It would waste a lot of time he wasn't sure he could afford. But he couldn't afford to be drygulched, either, and he was getting damned tired of being played for a fool.

There was a dip in the terrain just beyond the ragged outcrop and, once out of sight in the trough of this sink, Rafe turned the mare west at a lope, hauling his pack horse along willy-nilly.

He kept up this pace for almost a mile, watching the lather come out on Bathsheba, watching the dwindling height of the spine. The lowering sun pitched their shadows behind them, and in a far play of pale blues and purples now revealed a low huddle of hills off ahead that he had not previously been even vaguely aware of. He stopped again, peering narrowly, not learning a thing but rather nervously wondering if they were actually hills or piles of drifted sand like the dunes in which he had been found by Bunny's dad. He began to wonder if maybe these weren't the very ones.

Not that it greatly mattered. Sand can drift considerable distances if a big enough puff of wind gets under it, and the winds out here were freaky for sure. And he might have come farther behind this spine than he'd thought. The ridge was still with him, lower, less rugged, barely shielding him now from the view he'd abandoned.

With a yank at the lead rope he kneed Bathsheba again into motion. He didn't dare push them any more in this heat with the ground so heavy underfoot; without a horse in this country a man was soon dead. Going forward at a walk he kept one eye peeled for trouble while the other eye probed the mysterious hills which might prove, if he reached them, to be some weird trick of light and shadow, a mirage.

Suddenly Rafe went stiff in the saddle. A puff of smoke showed above those hills and, while he stared, another, and another. In alarm and fury he swore like a mule skinner as, twisting around, the eyes seeming about to pop from his head, he spied a standing column of smoke in the south.

It made no difference if these signals were the work of Indians or Spangler. They were talking about him!

He twisted the lead rope about the horn and kicked Bathsheba into a gallop. It wasn't the smoke he was afraid of, but the person or persons to whom it was sent. They might be riding now to block off both ends, to fix up an ambush that could bury him here!

He jerked Bathsheba's head around and in the cold sweat of panic stampeded straight south.

It was the mare that finally brought him to his senses. She abruptly set back on her heels and stopped. The ground dropped off into a lemon and brick-red crisscross of gullies and arroyos, a veritable badlands maybe ten miles across.

In a maze like that a man could lose not only his pursuers but himself as well. Rafe thought about this, knowing he didn't have much choice. It was only a question of time before, guided by those smokes, they would nab him. Down there the watchers couldn't point him out.

He took a good look around, fixing marks in his head. Then he threw in the steel and they were on their way. Bathsheba, snorting, showing her distrust, kept trying to hold back, but he forced her down. Slithering, twisting, at times even sliding, they reached the gulch floor in a scramble of rubble. The pack horse coughed in the swirling dust, and the mare, seeming frantic, almost unseated Rafe.

'Now, here!' he snarled, cuffing her laid-back ears, 'you'll go where I say whether you like it or not!' and gave her another jolt with the spurs.

Bathsheba snorted, fought her head, but when Rafe shook out a length of rope, the mare, who had sampled such persuasion before, abandoned her stand and trotted sullenly ahead. It was hotter than the hinges down at these lower levels; not a breath stirred and what there was smelled like metal coming off a blast furnace.

Rafe pulled his animals down to a walk. Now that he had managed to drop out of sight those watchers would likely be expecting him to head southeast; they would anyway if they were some of Spangler's crowd, because southeast was the shortest way to reach his father's ranch.

Rafe looked up. About another hour to sundown. The animals needed rest and he could do with some himself. When the walls twisted around to where the floor was draped in shadow Rafe got off Bathsheba, relieved the gelding of its pack and unsaddled the mare. Next thing he did was dig the carbine out and examine it; it wasn't what he'd asked for but it would serve till he could come onto something better.

He found the glass and tucked it into his waistband and checked the foodstuffs, flour and beans and salt and sowbelly. He found two boxes of shells and loaded the saddle gun, dropping the rest of the cartridges in his pockets. He checked his belt gun and then sat down with his back to a wall to better consider strategy and figure out his chances.

They'd be expecting him back. Nobody was in this thing for laughs. What they had going was too profitable and desperate to put up with the risk represented by Rafe. Next time he got in their way they would kill him—or damn well try! Duke, especially.

It was while he was moodily chomping salt pork that it come over Rafe he might not be giving this guy Spangler his due, might be selling him short. A man who could hold off Alph Chilton like he was, sure wasn't no kind to go stamping your boot at.

Spangler would be playing for keeps. Duke was into this up to his eyeballs, but Spangler was the one who'd be passing out the orders, and any guy smart as him would be too shrewd to think a feller who'd taken the beating they'd given Rafe would come charging back by the shortest route. Spangler would think Rafe had learned more caution. The one place they wouldn't be like to look for him now was the part of these badlands closest to the ranch. This decided, Rafe got busy. Within five minutes he was on his way, riding with the carbine ready across his knees. The shadows around him had thickened up considerable. Be some pretty tough *hombres* hanging out around the home place, but he would worry about these when he got to them. The big worry right now was getting out of this maze.

He kept turning left every time he reached a fork. Twice, going into blind canyons, he was forced to come back. It was full dark now with not much showing but the stars. Rafe reckoned he had come about five miles. It was fairly open here but he kept to a walk thinking he could better afford time than noise.

Another hour slipped by, then another thirty minutes. Rafe, by this time jumpy as a cat, began uneasily to wonder if he'd got turned around. Ground underfoot seemed to be still slanting down when, by his calculations, they'd ought to be climbing up out of this. Wall seemed to be pinching in again, too. What few stars he could see failed to offer any notion of which way he was pointed.

His disquiet grew. The mare, ears flat, moved as though she were trying to step between eggs. Now the ground commenced climbing in a spiraling twist, and there was a lot of cold air coming up through Rafe's pantslegs. In this swirling stillness the drop of each hoof was like a tiny explosion, the skreak and pop of straining leather scratching against Rafe's ears with all the stridence of a yell.

Bathsheba stopped, both ears jerking forward. Rafe, peering ahead, couldn't see a thing but the goddamn black that was everywhere about them. He could feel the mare tremble. With a shake of the head and a sudden snort she spun on bunched legs and would have frantically bolted if Rafe, hauling hard on the reins, hadn't stopped her. He reined her about and kicked with one heel.

Bathsheba squatted. You'd have thought, by grab, there was somebody up there!

It didn't make sense. This would be the east rim—some part of it; there hadn't been time for them to reach any other. This was the one place Spangler wouldn't be looking for him.

The mare was blowing like she had rollers in her nose. Catching hold of the lead rope he booted her again. Whickering, she went stiff-legged forward, her evident reluctance rankly steeped in distrust.

With the lead rope, his carbine and a balky mare to hold onto, Rafe had his hands full but kept going; and now, against the stars, he saw the rim's ragged lip. He could feel the mare stiffening up again. He let her stop and got out of the saddle. She stood there, trembling, ears flat against her head. The feel of this place tightened his grip on the carbine. It was too stinking still. Forced to believe he'd miscalculated somewhere he twisted the reins about the pommel so that if trouble was up there she wouldn't get tangled. He let go of the lead rope. With both hands damply clamped to the carbine he started cautiously putting one foot before the other.

Another three steps would have put his head above the rim when a stone twisted harshly under his boot. A rifle belted flame across the dark a yard above him. Someone viciously cursed. Behind Rafe, with a panicked snort, Bathsheba slammed into the pack horse. Squealing and kicking it was knocked off its feet, the wail of its whimper wildly diving through space as the mare, in a scramble of hoofs and loose rock, tore off down the backtrail like hell emigrating on cart wheels.

CHAPTER ELEVEN

With his belly squeezed flat against the wall's rotten rock, Rafe listened to the racketing of rifles being emptied so close he wondered they didn't take the top of his head off. In such a deafening bedlam there wasn't much chance for scuffing the wrinkles out of plans gone to pot. Like some rattlebrained kid he'd come bumbling right into Spangler's trap, and none of the things that were flapping inside him even remotely held out much hope.

The guns had quieted but their clamor was still caterwauling and tumbling around through the gulches. Left afoot against the face of the cliff, Rafe knew better than to imagine the bugger responsible was about to go off without a good look around.

His bunch was listening, stretching their ears to lay hold of Rafe's whereabouts. The stillness throbbed like a toothache. Then someone said, 'Hell! He's prob'ly piled up down at the bottom with them broncs.'

Spangler growled, 'I wouldn't bet on it. That peckerneck's got more lives than a cat! Get some brush stacked along the edge here.'

Boots tramped off, began scuffling around. It was hard for Rafe to stay where he was, never moving a finger, while his carbine got heavier and time inexorably moved nearer to the moment when inevitably they would find him. Yet to move was to bring the whole pack hellity larrup. He scarcely dared breathe with Spangler standing right over him. One false step, one sound...

With careful pressure, infinitesimally applied, a rounded stone from the wall came loose in his fingers and, with a silent prayer, he tossed it into the black that had swallowed his pack horse. About the time he was ready to burst from held breath, a rattle came up off the rocks far below. Flame came out of the dark above him. The crew came running.

'You see him?' Duke cried.

Spangler, not answering, said, 'Get that brush blazin'.'

'Ain't no brush,' grumbled one of the other. 'Couldn't find—'

'Get some of that dead grass then.'

'Think you got him?' That was Duke again.

'We're stayin' right here until we know for damn sure.'

Even if he could have found one Rafe wouldn't have risked plopping another rock down there. He thought of taking off his boots and trying to ease back down the trail, but the hazards looked worse than the risk of remaining; right now they thought he was down there. Boots clomped again. 'Brill,' Spangler growled, 'you and Fentriss light them grass twists. Rest of us'll clobber anything that moves.'

A fine kettle of fish! Rafe reflected, inwardly groaning. His fingers were giving him plenty of hell in this twenty degrees drop in temperature that often, in the thin air at this altitude, came with the bullbats and cricket chirps accompanying full dark. With a jumpy care he passed the carbine from aching right hand to cramped left, flexed the emptied fingers and dug out his belt gun.

It came to him then, with a crochety wonder, there must be a heap more behind what was happening than anyone so far had seen fit to mention. All this over a bunch of stole broncs! It just didn't seem natural. Not even the land—big as maybe it was, looked important enough to inspire so diverse and deadly an interest on the part of so many incompatible elements. A man's own kin telling him straight to his face—and his only sister who'd run after him barefooted clean to Beckston's Four Corners! And that saloon jasper, Dahl—where did he come in?

Chilton, the banker, you could understand. Even Duke. But the rest of it... Rafe, shaking his head, cautiously turned himself around, getting his back against the prods of the wall so that when those buggers started making a sieve of him he might, with luck, take a pair or three along.

It wasn't so dark now; the rim stood out against a brightening glow; and he braced himself, pistol lifting, belatedly remembering a number of things he had meant to take care of but never got around to; also fleetingly thinking with regret of things he might better never of put his hand to. Wisps of blazing grass came down, twisting and swirling as the fire ate into them, and hats appeared along the lip of the rim, the barrels of rifles with the light skittering off them.

But there weren't any shots. And Rafe, suddenly trembling, lowered his six-shooter, limp with the shock of execution postponed.

The why of it was evident, peering up with his mouth open. It wasn't lack of initiative on the part of Spangler's gunnies that found him still on his feet and still breathing; he was alive because sight was forced to travel a straight line. The rim overhung Rafe's placement a good arm's stretch. Even with the burning grass pushing the dark back, the rim's lip concealed him.

'Where is he?' Duke cried testily. Somebody else growled, 'There's his pack horse!' and Spangler said, 'He's down there someplace without he's got wings. We'll cover you, Brill. Go take a look.'

It got quiet again. Then Spangler cursed. 'Your feet froze, Brill, or is it jest your hearin'?'

'You think he's under that goddamn horse?'

'Send the Paiute.' That was Duke, brave as hell.

'All right, White-eye.' There was a shifting of feet, but nothing came of it. 'Your guts turned to fiddle strings, too?'

Spangler sounded like he was about fed

up, but the breed, apparently, didn't want any part of it. With grass burnt out the dark looked thicker than a buffalo coat. Spangler's voice, edged with fury, came impatiently through it. 'Duke, take Fentriss an' go round the other way. There's enough brush down there—'

'Not me,' Duke snarled. 'Who the hell you think you're talkin' to!'

You could feel the silence like a hand pushing at you. Then saddle leather skreaked, a horse moved off, and Rafe reckoned Spangler had gone himself. This did not greatly ease his tension or noticeably improve the look of his chances. Spangler, when he got into the gulch, would fire the brush, lighting up this trail like a barn afire. If Spangler couldn't see him—knowing Rafe couldn't watch two ways at once—one of those still up there with Duke likely could be induced to come down from above; or they might rush him. Rafe certain sure wouldn't want to wait for that.

Question was should he go up or down?

Below he might run into the range boss, above he would face a storm of lead. They must see this, too, and would expect him if he ran to try to get through below. No one but a wall-eyed drunk could hope to get by that bunch around Duke.

But if he tried to get back down into the roughs he was pretty near bound to be heard. With so much angry lead slashing around it was hard to see how all of it could miss him—and what about Spangler? A crack shot, probably, and knowing this range as Rafe never could. Looked like damned if he did and hell if he didn't.

Scowling, Rafe got out of his boots, removed their spurs and pushed them deep into his pockets. Looping the boots through his belt by their pull-straps he rebuckled it around him in such a manner the boots were held against his rump where they weren't so apt to go knocking into things. He looked again, long and wistful, in the direction his skewbald mare had bolted. Finally, clamping his jaws, he began gingerly picking his way toward the rim.

The cold shale-littered trail was hard on his feet. The quiet up on top where the crew stood waiting was even harder to endure, so greatly did the peril of discovery restrict each tentative impulse toward movement; and the strain got worse with every step put behind him.

He breathed a little freer when a murmured altercation briefly flared, but Duke's angry tones swiftly broke this up, Rafe having gained scarcely more than two yards. He still had about three more to go, and time was running out. If Spangler got his fire started before Rafe could manage to get over the lip, that old sweet chariot was going to swing low.

This was not a particularly comforting thought.

For close-in fighting—and it would be that kind if he had any chance at all—Rafe would have much preferred to depend on his belt gun. He found it awkward to be toting a weapon in each fist, and he damn sure wasn't about to throw away that carbine. He stuck the pistol into the front of his pants and then, bent double, put another yard behind him.

It was slow, sweaty work and any moment, he thought bitterly, that cold-jawed Spangler might get into the gulch and touch off the brush. Or one of them muttering pukes up above might take it into his nut to look over. Even if the guy couldn't see him he would have to be deaf, if he come that close, not to know somebody was moving right under him.

But nobody looked. There was no sound of boots. The Bender crew, evidently, was too indifferent, too lazy or too cautious to move out of their tracks. Weren't muttering now, either. Rafe, straining his ears till he thought they'd snap off, couldn't hear a dang thing; and his back was killing him.

He eased down on his knees, nerves screwed so tight they was like piano wires. He put down his saddle gun to flex cramped fingers and rub the damp off them. The rim was so near he could pretty near touch it; about a yard to go. He got to chewing his lip, trying to figure which was like to hold the most chance—to bust right on into them or try to wriggle through.

He was still on his knees, trying to make up his mind, when the black loom of the cliff face dissolved into flickering shadows.

Rafe didn't wait for any leaden translations. Scooping up his carbine, he surged to his feet and scrambled over the rim in one wild leap. He was among them before Spangler's hardcases got hold of their wits enough to know what was happening.

They were all afoot. The meaty impact of Rafe's carbine dropped one like a bursted sack, sent a second man staggering; then, like a swarm of hornets, they were all over him, swinging and swearing, clawing like wildcats to get him down. There wasn't enough room now to club with his carbine; Rafe smashed the butt of it into somebody's face, brought up his knee into the groin of another. This thinned them a little. Then someone leaped on his back, almost knocking him down. A hand reached and tore at his neck, and somebody's shoulder caught him hard in the chest. Gasping, he got all his strength together, bracing his feet, and whirled, the flying legs of the man on his back clearing a path. The man's strangling grip broke loose and he was gone.

But so was most of Rafe's strength. His knees began to wabble. Fists beat against his back and he reeled through a kind of red fog sprung from nausea. Blows seemed to rain on him from every direction. The carbine was torn from his hands. There was the warm slippery taste of salt in his mouth, and he knew this was blood; and in the brightening glare from the roaring brush he saw their hate-twisted faces and their hands closing in again.

He got the six-shooter out of the waistband of his pants and slashed its barrel across the nearest face, laying it open from jaw to ear. The flames threw back the lifting wink of metal in several other fists but, with so many of their fellows in such close proximity, no one it seemed wanted to fire the first shot. Rafe, on his knees, had no such scruples. His pistol barked and somebody yelled; he fired again and a man, twisted half around, went down with both hands clapped to his neck. Another gun went off, another man collapsed. Rafe, lunging up, dived into the welter of kicking, plunging horses, managing to nab one that had stepped on its reins.

Lead sang over his head as he tore off the bridle and hurled himself up. The panicked horse was going full stride before even Rafe's leg settled over the saddle. With an arm round its neck he yelled in its ear like a half-crocked Apache. The ground flew past, the wind whipped off his hat, the shouting gun-pierced racket of Duke's crew was left behind.

CHAPTER TWELVE

When Rafe got back enough wind and nerve to risk straightening up and having a look at his situation he must have been at least two miles north of the rim.

The thunder of hoofs which he'd thought was pursuit turned out to be several of the Bender crew's horses which, swept up in the excitement, had come along with him.

He got his mount stopped and, while the horse blew, took a long edgy squint at his backtrail. The star filled night loomed vast and empty; then a voice said, seemingly right at his elbow, 'Reckon I've growed enough gray hairs fer both of us!'

Rafe came around. The feller's dark shape wasn't a rope's throw away. He had his hands shoulder high and, though his chuckle was nervous, both of them looked empty. 'You won't need that artillery. I'm the jigger that he'ped you bust loose. Hell—' he said when Rafe made no move to put up his pistol, 'you sure didn't figger you done that all by yourself?'

Rafe, kneeing the captured horse in closer, growled, 'Who're you?'

'Just one of the Bills. You can call me "Brownwater"— ever'one else does.'

Now that he was up near enough to make out things, Rafe could see by the way he spread over his saddle the feller had enough extra fat hanging on him to do a whole tribe of Papagos half the winter. He looked mighty near big as Bunny's pa, Pike, and had a mottled appearance like he'd got in the way of an upended paint bucket—freckles, probably. He had a chaw in one cheek and a wheeze to his voice and seemed altogether as unfit for the part he claimed to have played as a two-legged dog in a three-ring circus. Rafe said, suspicious, 'How'd you get into this?'

'It's kind of a long story. I'm Lucy's beau. Was, anyways, till that brother of yours—'

'How'd you know I *had* any brother!'

Brownwater grinned. You could tell by the shine of his teeth. 'I was in that harness room back of the tree when you was tryin' that day to git the prodigal's hug an' Duke kep'—'

'If you was there,' Rafe growled, 'tell me who got the paper.'

'Duke grabbed it out of the Old Man's hand just before Spangler bended that gun over your head. Hell,' the fat man said with his look juning jumpily into the black, 'we better git whackin'!'

There was a whole heap of things Rafe was aching to know, but so long as he kept his eyes skinned and one fist wrapped about the handle of his shooter he reckoned it wouldn't hurt to ride a spell with this john. 'All right,' he grumbled, 'lead out an' stay careful.'

They pushed along at a lope, driving into the east for maybe three or four miles; then they eased up a bit bending south at a jog while the night got colder and a ground wind whined through the catclaw and pear.

When Brownwater pulled up to blow the horses Rafe had belted his pistol, had both hands in his pockets trying to thaw out the cramps. The fat man had his fists in plain sight, piled atop the horn of his saddle like they was hostages for good conduct. There wasn't anything to be heard but the wind, no thud of hoof pound, no whisper of shouts.

'Where are we?' Rafe asked.

'Gourd an' Vine. About four miles due north of headquarters. Figgered you'd be wantin' to auger some with your paw.'

Rafe's brows squeezed down. 'You hopin' to run me into a jackpot?'

'That bunch won't be along fer a while—'

'Says you!' Rafe jeered, and set the good hand to reaching back for his pistol.

The fat man sighed. 'If I'd wanted you flattened would I of he'ped you git clear?'

Rafe scowled. If he could only get hold of an end of this thing, get it straight in his head what all this was about. 'If you helped me, how come? You don't know me from Adam.'

'Have to be blind not to know you're a Bender. Sticks out all over you an', from what Lucy's said—'

'If you heard anything at all you heard her say Rafe's dead!'

It was Bill's turn to frown. 'She had her reasons. Man, you got to trust *someone*. Nobody can go it alone in this world! People, the most of 'em, ain't as bad as you think. You got to give them a chance. Lucy and me, we was fixin' to git married till Duke put his foot down—'

'Duke!' Rafe snorted. 'It wasn't for *him* to say.'

'Looks like he's kinda dim in your memory. Duke aims to git what Duke wants—even if he has t' bury half the golrammed county. He was powerful persuasive.'

Some of what Brownwater Bill went on to say was admittedly guesswork, but certain cold facts were pretty readily apparent. Spangler, a holy terror with a gun, and about the hardest formation a man was like to bump into, had been caught red-handed running off Bender horses. He'd been come onto by Rafe's brother and the banker, Alph Chilton, which same had lost no time getting out of that neighborhood. From this day on you couldn't have lured Chilton out of town on a bet.

That Duke was still enjoying good health, and Spangler still bullypussin' round as Bender range boss, was cause for considerable guarded talk and wonder, the more so since on the face of things the ranch was losing more stock than ever; was indeed in rather desperate plight with bills piled on bills and none of the merchants—not even the bank—being able to collect a thin dime on account.

Brownwater had it there'd been a deal, and Rafe guessed there probably had; though one might think, all things considered, it would have left Spangler cracking the whip. Such, by Brownwater's tell, was not the case. Duke was in the driver's seat and steering the ranch hellbent for ruin.

'Ain't a lick of sense to it,' the fat man declared. 'Scowl an' growl till you're blue in the face, you can't make it stand up. But it does—it surely does! All the old hands is gone, all but me. Crew they got now is saltier'n Lot's wife, and with them kinda fellers it's cash on the barrelhead. I've thought mebbe the stole broncs is bein' sold over Duke's writin', but with all these toughs they got to pay an' feed where does Spangler come off? Now *you* tell *me*.'

'I can't,' Rafe scowled, and this was purely the truth. 'I can't even see how come—if they run all the rest of the old bunch off an'

Duke don't want you sweet-talkin' Luce—you're still on the spread an' still above ground.'

'Chafes a mort of wear off a feller's mental axle, but I can tell you how one part of it's worked,' Brownwater wheezed with a gusty sigh. 'Spangler wants Luce, has threatened to ventilate my carcass if I even so much as open my mouth to her. Duke has been more or less keepin' him in line by promising she'll be Spangler's wife the day Duke gits full title to Gourd an' Vine. He's got Luce believin' the first time she crosses him I'll be turned into a colander an' she'll be turned over to Spangler. It's enough t'cramp rats but, believe me, it works.'

The fat man hitched at his pants and spat gloomily. 'Expect we better be shakin' some dust.'

Rafe had put on his boots. Now he buckled on his spurs and kneed the Bender horse after Brownwater Bill. He would sure like to know what had happened to Bathsheba. A man hates to give up the things he's been used to.

As they rode on through the night the fat man's words kept tramping through his head in confusing tangle; even after he'd got them all pawed over, and got their gist about digested, there were gaps enough to drive a ten-mule hitch through. You could only assume that there were pieces still missing.

No kind of threat from any pipsqueak like Duke was going to put much weight on a hard chunk like Spangler. The man would laugh in his face! It didn't look like, either—no matter how fierce an itch the guy might have for their sister, the promise of Luce, by itself, would put him to sawing second fiddle for Duke.

There had to be something else, something more, something Spangler would want to get his hands on even worse and which, at least so far, had been kept out of his reach.

It was just beginning to get light enough to see by—everything fused in dreary shadings of gray—when they caught their first glimpse of the buildings. Brownwater nodded his head. 'Half a mile.' He spat out his tobacco. 'Shouldn't be no trouble unless they recognize you. Duke left two of Spangler's gunnies on tap in case the Ol' Man or Luce got minded t' hunt greener pasters.' He tugged his hat lower over his eyes. 'I'll lead the way.'

Rafe's jaws tightened. That whole business back yonder—every last lucky part of it—could have been play-acted for Rafe Bender's special benefit. Duke was wily as a goddamn fox! And even if it wasn't, this self-styled 'Lucy's beau' could be working hand in glove with one of them to lead Rafe up like a lamb for the slaughter. Why'd he spit out his chaw! *Was that tug he'd give to his hat a signal?*

Rafe dropped back and let him have his way. Like Brownwater had said, a feller had to trust *some*one. When things started coming apart at the seams it was easy to imagine every gent and his uncle had a knife out for you. He'd been sure old Pike and that flossy-looking Bunny had been fixing to do him dirt. Made him flush now just to remember it. And he had given Spangler credit for greater savvy than he'd shown, so sure he wouldn't be up on that bluff he had dang near run right into him.

But he didn't have to foller this guy with his eyes shut!

He rubbed some warmth into his fist and took hold of his pistol, determined if this was a trap to make it cost them dear. With the other, stiffer hand he got the chin-strapped hat back onto his head, hauling down the brim to put his cheeks in deeper shadow. There wasn't much else he could do but keep his eyes peeled.

Rafe's guide, without turning his head, said abruptly, 'Duke's had the runnin' of this spread fer two years. He's *aimin'* to have it lock, stock an' barrel. Ain't nothin' he won't do except mebbe kill the Old Man outright an', if things gits rough, he could do that, too.'

Worst of it was, the guy was probably

right. Duke, in the past, had never let anything stand in the way when it came to something he figured he wanted. He was antigodlin, mean and revengeful. He might do a heap of backing and filling but there was also, deep in the hateful twisted core of him, a frightening persistence once he'd made up his mind. He hadn't no more scruples than a goddamn pistol.

Before he did anything else, Rafe guessed, he had better get Luce and his dad away from here.

When he looked up again they were coming into the bare open of the yard, if you could call this one. The grim fortress-like house, with its windowless outside walls, its parapets and ramparts, loomed dark and deserted. The walking hoofs of their horses sounded loud to Rafe as the clash of cymbals. But no one hailed. The tangle of pens showed bars down and empty.

Brownwater Bill, with his hat cuffed back, rode bold as you please to the great open gate and sat there, impassive, waiting for Rafe to come up. Inside he might be tore up as a breaking pen but his face anyway, in this leaden light, looked calm as a millpond. No matter which way he swung, the guy had guts. You had to give him that.

Rafe wished he could feel as sure of his own.

As he stopped his horse just back of the

other a gunhung hardcase packing a rifle stepped out of the room to the right of the gate and, with a careless flap of the hand, was about to wave them on in when something about Rafe's look suddenly stiffened him. He sucked a lungful of air, his whole face springing open. Before he could yell or get his rifle fully up, Brownwater, diving from his saddle, came down on the feller like a ton of dropped meat. When Lucy's beau, panting, got up off the man, Spangler's hardcase was trussed hand and foot with twists of piggin' string snatched from Bill's belt, mouth stuffed with shirt tail, eyes looking wilder than a pulque-drunk squaw's.

'Inside quick!' Brownwater wheezed, pawing around for his pistol.

A crack from Rafe's heel propelled his mount through the gate. Brownwater, dragging his horse, was quick to follow. As Rafe swung down, the fat man, whacking his animal out of the way, hurried back to catch hold of the gate. A gun went off, that slug striking the wood not an inch from his hand.

Rafe, spinning, felt a tug at his hat as the gun spoke again. Then Rafe's own pistol coughed. Across the patio a black-bearded six-footer wheeling out of a door hole jerked half around, flung out a fist and went down.

Brownwater, slamming shut the massive gate, skreaked a bar through the slots and let out a gusty 'Whew!' as old Bender appeared, and Luce—white-cheeked and frantic—came flying to fling herself into Bill's arms.

'There, there,' Brownwater mumbled, looking sheepish and tickled, trying awkwardly to pat her as he would a frightened filly. 'Nothin' to git your wind up over—'

She cried indignantly, 'You might have been killed!'

Rafe, starting toward his father, never heard another word. One foot up and one foot down, he stopped in midstride, all the breath knocked out of him.

CHAPTER THIRTEEN

Flabbergasted, jaw flopping, he stared like a snake had suddenly reared in his path. He let the lifted foot down with a blurted 'Godlemighty!'

A delicious, humorously infectious laugh tumbled out of Bunny as she watched his scandalized stare take in her man's hickory shirt and the belted, washfaded, brush-snagged Levi's that so fondly clung to her lithe, shapely legs. 'Is that all you can dig up to say?'

Rafe gulped, red-faced, and his eyes swiveled away; and old Bender said in patient perplexity, 'Is that you, Duke? What is she laughing at?'

Rafe didn't know if he were more upset by her brazen appearance or the gall of her presence. He was mad clear through. What did she think she was up to anyway, tagging him around like—like a dang fool squaw!

A clatter of hoofs broke across his harsh thoughts; and Bender now said with some asperity, 'Will somebody tell me what's goin' on?'

Brownwater, climbing down off the gate, muttered, 'Cook's pulled out,' and the old man's staring eyes flopped around like a couple of hounds that had overshot the trail. 'He's gone for Duke and Spangler,' Luce said, again catching hold of Brownwater's arm.

Bender's eyes found her face; and Bunny, speaking out when nobody else would, told him bluntly, 'They've been off chasing your heir—your son, Rafe.'

The craggy head came around in a wild, lost look, the groping eyes trying to find her. Ineffably sad, he said, 'You're mistaken. Rafe was killed in the war—'

'That's what they *want* you to think! He's back from the war. They've been out there all night trying to catch him and kill him. It's what I came here to tell you. But Luce was afraid; Duke said if she crossed him he'd turn her over to Spangler—ask Brownwater

128

there. *He'll* tell you! They intend for Duke to come into this property—'

'It's his right,' Bender said.

'Rafe was your first son; it should go to Rafe!' Bunny cried. 'He's right here with you now—'

'Stop!' Bender's voice was the squawk of an eagle. The blind eyes turned fierce. 'Is there nothing you Yankees won't do! Chilton claiming I've mortgaged this place! You Pikes trying to foist an imposter—I told your father when he came here the first time Rafe was killed in the war.'

'But he wasn't! He's here! Not ten steps away from you. Say something, Rafe!'

Rafe licked dry lips. 'That's right, Pa. I'm here.'

For an agony of time Bender stood like a stone. It got so quiet in the courtyard if you had closed your eyes you'd have sworn the place was empty. The sun's lifting face yellowly brightened the west wall and the chirping of birds came sweet and clear, yet no one moved. The trembling lips of the patriarch, firming, cried, 'That's the voice of the one who was out here before!'

'Certainly. Rafe,' Bunny said. 'Don't you know your son's voice?'

'Be still,' Bender said, his tone curt with scorn. 'Rafe's was never so deep—'

'You're remembering a boy, he's a grown man now.'

Luce, coloring, said, 'It *is* Rafe, Pa.'

The staring eyes came about. 'You said it wasn't, before.'

'I know. God forgive me.' Her pleading look went to Rafe, shy and shamed.

'She was scared,' Rafe said. 'I don't hold it against her.' He pushed the gun into his belt. 'This son that you say is dead—did he have any mark by which you might know him? Somethin', I mean, that—'

'Of course! The mole," Luce said. 'You remember the mole, Pa.'

Brownwater said, 'We ain't got much time,' but he might as well not have spoken for all the notice Rafe gave. He was watching Bender.

Hope had come into the old man's face. Though the doubt still showed, there was a surging excitement in the turn of his head. 'I remember it well. Put my hand on it, boy.'

Rafe shrugged out of his shirt. He walked over to Bender. He said, faintly grinning, 'Which side was it on?'

Bender stiffened. 'Was under his right arm, just above the elbow.'

Rafe reached out the arm. 'All right. Put your hand on it. Then tell me Rafe's dead.'

Brownwater, back on the gate, softly swore. 'There's a dust out there. We better git whackin'.'

Bender, with his hand on the mole, was saying 'Boy! Boy!' sounding all choked up, his other arm tugging Rafe hard and fierce. Great tears brimmed and spilled unheeded down his wrinkled cheeks; the girls were weeping also. Brownwater, disgusted, caught hold of Rafe and shook him. 'I don't want t' break nothin' up, but if you ain't fixin' t' be a dead hero you better give some mind t' how we're to git outa here.'

Seeming at last to get through to him, Rafe, giving the old man a final squeeze, disengaged himself, and, stepping back, said with his own eyes smarting, 'Bill, you get the horses. We'll—'

'What horses!' The fat puncher, cramming a fresh chew into him, worked his jaws, spat grimly and growled, 'You seen them pens! Only nags in sight is the ones we come in on. How far you figure we'd git on them?'

Luce knuckled her eyes. 'There's four of you. That's two to a mount, and Rafe—'

'I'm stayin' right here.'

'Don't be a boob!' Bunny flared, glaring at him. 'If you're going to stay we may as well *all* stay! Now get that silly grin off your face and, while Luce packs some grub—'

'No time fer that,' Brownwater cut in. 'That bunch ain't scarcely five minutes away.'

'These walls are thick,' Luce said. "Why run? We've got food and water.'

While the rest were considering, eying each other, Brownwater said, 'Food can run out, and when our guns is shot dry what do we use? Time ain't goin' to be no help to us.' He put his meaningful stare on Bender.

'You're right,' Bunny sighed. 'Get that gate open. I'll not be a minute.' Whirling, ducking the well curb, she ran off through the pepper tree's green ferny lace, reappearing moments later tugging a big roan horse whose reins she thrust hurried into Rafe's hands. 'You take Roanie—he's freshest. I'll get up with your father.' Brownwater, dragging open the portal with Luce's nervous help, shouted, 'Never mind us—they're goin' t' take after *you*! Look for us where you lost the skewbald. Git goin'!'

Rafe, still reluctant, and showing it, climbed aboard Bunny's horse, meaning to argue this further. While his weight was yet on the stirrup, the big puncher, yelling, fetched the blue roan a clip with his hat. The horse took off like a bat out of Carlsbad, the swearing Rafe becoming too busy trying to stay with him to have any breath or time left for gab.

Off to his left as he sailed through the gate a bedlam of furious shouts went up, but he hadn't any attention he could spare them, either. When he got his seat firmly sunk in the saddle and had found his other stirrup he sneaked a quick look and gave the roan back his head. There was six or eight of them pouring in the steel and laying on the leather in a frantic attempt to cut him off before he could pass that tangle of pens.

But all the shouting and shooting only increased the roan's fright. Pinning back his ears he really stretched out and his few hours of rest began to pay off. He tore past the pens in a wild burst of speed. Slowly but surely he began pulling away, opening up his lead a little more with every stride.

The pursuit quit firing but they kept on coming, falling farther behind, plainly determined not to quit until they had to. Duke had never given a damn about horseflesh. Rafe guessed Spangler was riled enough to chew carpet tacks. They would kill him, all right, if they ever glommed onto him.

It was obvious now it would not be today. Some of their crew had already pulled up and the most of the others were strung out half a mile. Only Spangler and Duke, on the best of their horses, were still in the race, still spurring and quirting with the fury of frustration; Rafe, with a laugh, gleefully pictured their faces.

He grew sober in a hurry when the rhythm of the roan's hard run commenced to falter. Rafe switched him into a gallop, then a lope. When the ride continued rough he dropped him into a jog. The reaching lunge of his breath was like a bellows. Greatly concerned—even worried, now—Rafe peered behind and, a mile away, saw the pair still after him, indomitable as death.

He was afraid for his lead to ease the horse any further. If they again managed to get within saddle gun range they would probably drop off, do their level best to nail him. He kept the roan going, talking to him now, pleading with him, coaxing, promising oats and turnip greens, anything and everything that came into his head. The lather, on chest and flanks, showed like soap, and Rafe could no longer doubt the horse was limping.

With bitterness he pulled up and jumped down, reaching for the scabbarded rifle. Then he stared, stared again. The day had considerably advanced, the sun being presently almost straight over head in the full powers of its strength, but astonishingly, and in spite of this brilliance, he could find no sign of Spangler or Duke. If they hadn't given up they had at least dropped out of sight.

Rafe picked up the roan's feet. When he got to the off front hoof he found the trouble. A sharp, three-cornered stone had tightly wedged in the frog. While it wasn't by any means a case for shooting, it was a cinch the roan would carry him no farther, not without Rafe irreparably ruining him.

Rafe dug the stone out. The animal would be of no use for several days. Rafe scowled about, trying to find some landmark that would fix his location. But this was all new country to him. Unknown. Haired over with last year's yellow grass it gently rolled toward a blue blur of hills back over his left shoulder which *might* be the ones that hid his father's headquarters. Where was the old man now? And the girls? Had Brownwater got them out of there?

Rafe's scowl deepened. Since he wasn't able to see any cattle it seemed a likely assumption he was probably still on Gourd and Vine range. And if those hills hid the ranch—he couldn't see any others close enough to matter—the rendezvous where he'd lost Bathsheba must be some place west, how far he had no notion. But a powerful long way for a man to have to go in high-heeled boots.

He picked up the reins, clucked to the roan and started walking.

The horse didn't balk but after an hour of increasing heat Rafe stopped to pull off the saddle and blanket; then with handfuls of grass he rubbed the roan down. Retrieving the rifle, he looked a long time at the saddle before abandoning it; he caught up the canteen, filled his hat with the tepid water and let the horse drink. Taking up the reins once more, he again moved west.

One thing he hoped more than anything else: that, at least, he was headed in the right direction. It wasn't himself he was worried about as much as it was the Old Man and the girls. If Duke and Spangler came onto them now things could get pretty sticky.

The sun heeled lower, the sharpening shadows dancing farther behind. Like romping dogs, Rafe wearily thought as, at ever-widening intervals, his reddened eyes sought the backtrail. His swollen feet ached miserably, then it got so they didn't seem part of him any more, more like something tied on he had to pull against his will. This got him thinking of horses, and he began to consider getting back on the roan. But this unaccountably clashed with some unexplainable ingrained concept he could neither unravel nor shake the shame out of; it surely did gravel him. 'What the hell's a horse for!' He heard himself shouting like some zany old fool. He also discovered he had finally quit sweating, and this scared him into some semblance of sanity.

★   ★   ★

He quit walking to think, but all he could think of was getting off his blistered feet. The only sensible answer was right behind him. He twisted his head and took a furious look. Abruptly—to make sure he bested temptation—he peeled the roan's bridle and pitched it away. When his eyes wouldn't leave it, he stomped the tooled leather out of sight in the sand.

Then he set off again.

Peering into the orange blaze of the sun he couldn't find the hills he'd picked out for steerage. *The blue hills of home.* The wistful sound of it made him curse. He thought of getting out of his boots, abandoning them, like the saddle and the bridle and the emptied canteen. His feet were so swollen he couldn't get the boots off. He couldn't bear to cut them so he went stumbling on.

The hills swam into his thinking again. He made a dogged search and saw them grayly back of him, away off to the south. He had to wrestle this around a while before he got the sense of it, before he was able to realize he must have come farther than he'd been minded to suppose. He hopefully reflected he was probably not more than a couple of miles off his goal—that eastern drop to the floor of the roughs where he'd lost Bathsheba and where Brownwater Bill had said they would meet. Not even the astonishing discovery of the crazy staggering look of his tracks was able entirely to eradicate the notion.

He could be very near. This was rough-looking country filled with swirls of fluted sand, the very convolutions of which might tend to hide from a man afoot any sign of the drop-off until he reached its brink. He began to look for the churned-up area where he'd made his fight and, with Brownwater's help, had escaped from the crew.

He couldn't find even one hoofprint, but in this surge of restored confidence refused to be shaken. Wind could have done that. He floundered on, topping ridge after ridge, his burning eyes encountering nothing but the mauve look of more sand ahead with the sun squatting on it like a disc of molten copper. He wouldn't let himself believe he was lost, not even when outcrops of rock began occasionally to show like broken ribs among the dunes.

Once, remembering the roan, he took another backward look, but the horse was gone, vanished in the immensity of darkening desolation. The air was still furnace hot. His throat was cotton dry. A terrible thirst began to plague him, cutting through all other miseries.

The sun's face was half-buried when he dragged the chin off his chest to go staggering on with his tatters of hope. In its failing light something clutched at his shins. He thought the land fell away until he felt the grate of sand between his teeth and realized it was only himself that had fallen. God, what luxury to be perfectly still! The blessed peace of resignation—but resignation was surrender. Another name for death.

He struggled onto an elbow, scowling back at the tangled look of his legs and the outcrop of rotten rock that had spilled him. With a sense of outrage he said: 'Son of a—!' and stopped, jaw sagging, his eyes about ready to pop from his head.

He clawed onto his knees and scrabbled back to the rock. When at last he stood up he was shaking all over. Like a man half asleep his fixed stare quartered the land. He had no remembrance of picking anything up but a chunk of the rock was in his hand. The rifle he'd been carrying was completely forgotten when he faced west again to go stumbling on.

It was almost full night when he came out on the rimrock and saw the dark gulf of the badlands below. Nothing stirred down there. No sound came up. The cliff-hung trail where he'd lost Bathsheba might be north of him or south. It was nobody's guess, and too stinking black to tell if the ground was scuffed or not.

Out of desperation he did a crazy thing. From a creosote bush he stripped an armful of branches, packed them back to the edge of the rim and put a match to them. It was a calculated risk. He had known the moment he found the bush he was in the wrong place, because where he had tangled with the Bender crew there had been no wood—they had had to use grass; and there was no grass here, only a few stunted bushes.

With a fascinated, more-than-half-defiant

dread, he watched flames leap from the resinous branches, orange and blue, the explosive colors of grease. On this bare lip they could be seen for miles. Would they fetch Spangler's gunhawks or Brownwater Bill?

CHAPTER FOURTEEN

They found him, all right.

This fat wood burned fast. He had to scurry about in the jump of his shadow, pulling up more bushes or see the blaze die before he got any good from it. When he ran out of the finger-thin branches the fire burned down to a bed of bright coals. But he kept on moving, around and around the still-red eye of it, knowing the need to make sure he was seen.

Spangler, Duke and company, if they saw and had managed to get hold of fresh mounts, would investigate whether he showed himself or not; but Brownwater, having Bender and the girls on his mind, would likely prove more cautious. He would have to see Rafe before he'd risk coming in. So Rafe kept tramping, half out of his head with the wear and the strain of it and scared, by God, the man would run anyway.

He was afraid even to think what he would

do if Bill did. In his present shape, afoot, without water and half starved besides, armed only with a belt gun and so dang bone-weary he could scarcely stand up, he'd have no more chance than a June frost in hell's kitchen.

He heard the strike of shod hoofs on stone, and whirled, stumbling away from the coals, snatching his pistol as he plunged into the blackness.

'That you, Rafe?'

It came up from below, Rafe almost collapsing in the shock of relief. It had to be Brownwater—nobody else wheezed like that.

An unreasoning anger rushed tumultuously through him, all he had undergone feeding this fury as he pictured Bill lallygaggin' with the girls, comfortable and safe as a frolic of church mice. Filled with it he growled, 'Get 'em on up here an' hurry it up!'

The shod hoofs going away, squandered no time in stealth. Rafe dropped, utterly spent, yet too feverishly filled with the whirl of his emotions to take any rest from it. He was up again pacing, when in the enfolding grip of deep quiet, hoofs pocked the night somewhere off to the left. One of the approaching animals nickered, and he came around, staring, on stiffening hips, certain even in the thick of this black there were more than two horses. He listened, canted forward, mouth open, heart thudding.

'It's only us,' Bunny said, so calm he could have shouted. 'Bill found your mare, and most of the grub that went off with your pack horse. Why don't you build that fire up a little?'

Why didn't he go stick his goddamn head in it! Rafe said, furious, 'We're headin' for town—'

'Town!' Brownwater bleated like a scalded pig. 'Gawd a'mighty! Sun cooked your brains, boy?' and Luce cried bitterly, 'Alph Chilton—'

'There's bigger things than Alph Chilton involved!' He could see well enough to know the mare when she nuzzled him. He reached for the horn, then stepped back. 'You'll ride with me,' he grumbled at Bunny.

'Ride with yourself,' Bunny said. 'I'm comfortable.'

Rafe stared.

Luce said, 'Somebody has to be up there with Pa,' and Brownwater nodded, 'He's about done in.'

Bunny, peering about, wanted to know what Rafe had done with her gelding. She didn't sound like she was minded to be put off.

'He went lame,' Rafe said. 'I pulled your gear and turned him loose.' He took the reins from Bill and, hauling Bathsheba's head around, pulled himself up, so gut sick and weak he thought for a minute he'd go straight on over. Breathing hard he hung to the horn with both hands.

'I can't see,' Luce complained, 'why you'd want to go to town. That's the first place they'll—'

'Don't argue about it, just do like I say. Important thing now is to get there,' Rafe muttered. He got his head up, tried to straighten his shoulders. 'Lead the way will you, Bill? Let's get started.'

The fat puncher said, 'You don't look too good. Maybe Lucy better ride with your pa and let Bunny—'

Bunny's snort cut him off. 'He don't need no help! What you trying to do—insult him? He's got a cast-iron hide and solid bone for a head! You might as well argue with the shadow of death. Go on and do what he says before he bows up and cuffs you.'

The two girls exchanged looks. Brownwater, scowling, said, 'Ahr—' but set off. Luce, behind with the knees sticking out of her hiked-up skirt, muttered, 'Who does he think he is—Julius Caesar!'

Rafe waited with his mouth hard shut until Bunny, wheeling past with his father, fell in behind Bill. Then Rafe turned Bathsheba into their tracks, so hungry he was dizzy, so dry in his throat he couldn't have said anything that would have half done him justice even could he have shoved it through the things that were choking him. He had all he could do to keep himself in the saddle.

An indefinable while later Brownwater spoke out of the black at his elbow. 'Lucy figgered mebbe you might want somethin' in your belly.'

It wasn't quite a question, not even noticeably apologetic; it was, however, an overture and, after staring hard at the blobs of their faces, Rafe, still silent, pushed out a hand. The girl put a leathery something into it. 'I—I'm sorry about what I said,' she mentioned, leaning out from her perch behind fat Bill to slip a weighted strap over his wrist.

The strap was attached to a near-empty water bag. After he'd squeezed the last drop out of it Rafe peered at the chunk of dried meat she'd put into his fist. He got it all down and perked up enough to take a harder look at the things on his mind, the more urgent ones at any rate. Likely, as Luce had pointed out, town was the first place Spangler would head for. Whether he got caught or not, Rafe had to go there. It was the only chance he could see to put a crack in their plans, and he wasn't naive enough to underestimate his peril. Spangler or Duke would shoot him on sight—he had no doubt of that. Even Chilton's sheriff.

But the only alternative was to let these buggers get away with it, and he sure couldn't see himself doing that. He wondered what price Jack Dahl had for his part. It must have been a pretty because at least the start of this deal had been set up with his connivance.

The night began to grow a little gray about the edges. Most of the stars had gone. A smell of rain was in the air; the smell of death was in it, too. Unconsciously Rafe shivered.

When first light finally came, they weren't more than a mile and a half from town. The sky was overhung with clouds but the land behind looked grayly empty. Rafe peered hard without discovering movement, but wasn't building no hopes on that. Spangler, if they'd got hold of fresh horses, could have sent some of his gunnies on ahead while Duke and the rest started hunting for tracks. One thing sure—they'd have horses by now. And if they'd followed his tracks to where he'd left Bunny's Roanie they would have the whole story. Duke might of run, but not that guy Spangler!

Chilton wouldn't be at his bank this early; yet this was where Rafe was determined to see him. He pushed it around for a while in his head. They could see the town's roofs across the tops of the trees growing out of the bosque into which Rafe had fled when Spangler's gunhand took after him. He thought some more, scowling, then abruptly called, 'Bill! You got any lawyers around here?'

'Only lawyer closer than Tucson,' Bunny said, 'is Alph Chilton.'

Rafe swore.

'If it's legal advice you're in need of,' said Brownwater, 'you could ride to Camp Grant an' put it up to the military—'

'I've got to get this done before Spangler—'

'Daddy's a notary,' Bunny said, watching him.

Rafe, even yet, wasn't sure he trusted Pike, but he didn't have much choice—not if he was to make his father safe. What he had in mind held some risk for Luce, but he couldn't help that. He had to act while he could. He got them into the trees where the limbs and leaves hid them, hauled Bunny off the old man's horse, helped Bender down; then, ignoring her spluttering, thrust the reins in her hands. 'Go get him. We'll wait right here.'

Choking back whatever she'd been going to say, she got into the saddle and rode off through the brush. Some things about her you simply had to admire.

The others got down; Luce, female fashion, putting store on appearance, trying to cuff some of the dust and wrinkles from her clothes. 'Whatever you two have got up your sleeves, I hope—'

Rafe said, cutting in, 'All we got to do is

cinch our hulls on this critter,' and tossed Brownwater the chunk of rock he'd picked up. The fat puncher took one look and whistled. It was hard to keep still after that but he done it. Luce, all agog, kept reaming him with her stares and, when this failed to unlock his lips, stuck her nose in the air and gave him her back. Rafe watched the town through their lattice of branches.

He'd about given Bunny up and, in a lather of impatience, was getting ready to move when she came up through the brush without her pa, and afoot. 'You don't need to swear,' she said, eying Rafe's scowl. 'Daddy's coming. In the buggy. He's gone around by the road.'

Rafe helped his father into the skewbald's saddle, grabbed hold of her cheekstrap and set off, the rest following. He could hear Luce back of him dinging at Bill, and the snapping of the brush and the hoofs of the horses coming through the leafy mold. 'We're making enough racket,' Bunny said, 'for a herd of elephants.' Things quieted down after that and Luce quit talking.

Rafe stood listening at the edge of the growth. All of them stopped when they saw him put a hand up, and the skreak and rattle of an approaching vehicle rumbled plainly off the planks bridging the gully at the edge of town. Rafe got Bender off Bathsheba. 'You an' Pa,' he said to Bunny, 'will ride in the buggy. Soon as you're aboard have Pike turn it round an' head for the bank. Luce—'

'Don't you think,' his father said a bit testily, 'I'm old enough to be told what you're up to? Seems like I ought to have some say—'

'You'll have plenty of say when we get to it. Right now we've got to have a talk with that banker. We've got to get to him 'fore Spangler shows up.' Rafe turned to his sister. 'Luce, you get on Bill's horse and go after Chilton. He's prob'ly still in bed—you know where he lives?'

Big-eyed, she nodded.

'Get goin', then.' He shoved her toward Bill's horse.

'But what will I tell him?'

'Tell him anythin'. Tell him the Old Man's waitin' with the money to pay off that mortgage. I don't care what you tell him, long as you fetch 'im. An' don't lallygag around pickin' no posies!'

Brownwater said, eying Rafe uneasily, 'I'm not sure I like this. Somebody could get bad hurt—'

'You got a better idea?'

'What's the matter with me goin' after him?' Bill said, reaching a hand out to Luce.

'If Spangler shows, I'm going to need your gun.'

They stared at each other. 'You're leanin' on a mighty weak reed,' the fat man said, but he dropped the hand. Luce climbed into the saddle. She put her horse through the trees.

Rafe stepped out and Pike pulled up, Bunny and Rafe helping Bender aboard, Pike wanting to know what this was all about. 'Drive 'em back to the bank and stay in the buggy—all of you—till Chilton shows up,' Rafe told him shortly. 'An', if lead gets to flyin', keep your heads down, but get into that bank no matter what.'

He slapped the horse on the rump and, as Pike wheeled for the turn, moved back into the brush. Gathering the skewbald's reins he lifted a foot to the stirrup. 'Let's go,' he growled, and swung into the saddle.

Brownwater, still looking kind of huffy, stood with his fat holding him anchored in his tracks. 'I'm beginnin' to feel like your ol' man—'

'Beginnin' to look like him, too. C'mon, let's get outa here,' Rafe said impatiently. 'We ain't got all day.'

Bill reluctantly forked the horse Rafe's father had been sharing with Bunny, grunting and grumbling as he pulled himself up, scowling like a Piegan squaw as he turned the horse in a walk after Rafe's. 'You figger t' wait out back'n the bank?'

When he got no answer to that, he said, 'Why can't we do this someplace else? There's lots of better —'

Rafe, twisting around, growled, 'I can

think of some places I'd rather be, too, but we got to get into that golram safe.'

Bill's jaw dropped. 'Now look here,' he wheezed, all choked up with emotion. 'I didn't hire out t' stick up no bank!' He hauled his horse to a stop, sat glaring.

'You want to marry my sister?' Rafe said, real soft.

The fat man stared as though confronted with a snake. When he began to swell up Rafe said, eyes hard, 'I'll be waitin'. Fetch Chilton's tin-badge an' be there in ten minutes.'

Swinging around in the saddle, Rafe rode off.

CHAPTER FIFTEEN

Waiting, Rafe decided, was the hardest thing a man had to do. Long as a feller could keep himself busy he went along pretty well, but give him time to think and all that kept him up began flying apart. Doubts crowded in, his nerves got to jangling, every joint in his carcass seemed about to give way. If he could only get down and stretch out.

He didn't dare. It was all he could do to stay awake as it was. His eyes felt like they'd been rolled in sand. His face was numb, his feet were twin screaming lumps of misery.

Every muscle in his body was a separate ache, jerking and twisting like a skillet full of eels; and any moment, he knew, this early morning quiet might explode into gunplay.

He damn near screamed just thinking about it.

Where was Spangler, and his brother, and their gun-hung crew? They'd come storming in sure as God made little apples! No matter how many risks he put in their way, Spangler, he was certain, wasn't going to be stopped this side of a bullet.

Duke was the weak one, always spinning like a weathercock, wanting things he had no right to, squirming, twisting, hating, scheming. Yet in this very weakness there was a desperate kind of conscienceless strength that could be harder than iron. It took a pretty cold fish to plot his own father's death; and that was what it amounted to, tying his kite to a guy like Spangler, helping the man put the ranch on the skids, determined no matter what to wrest it away from the owner of record. Probably, in the beginning, Duke—with Rafe out of the way—had figured to heir it. Must have been a considerable shock to have the true heir walk in on him that way, just when the place was pretty near in his pocket.

The Bender range boss was a different breed. Rafe would have bet good dollars against doughnuts he'd no intention of sharing anything. His kind never shared. Once Duke's use was exhausted Spangler, without the slightest compunction, would be rid of him. A bullet in the back was the best Duke could look for. But a man couldn't tell him that.

Rafe, discovering the trend of this thinking, snorted in disgust. He'd *done* his share of worrying over Duke; just the same it was a habit he found hard to get shed of. Hauling up a leg, still scowling, he got down. He had things more important to sweat about than Duke. It was time he got at them!

Keeping hold of the reins he limped over to the corner and had a look at the street. It was still too early for anyone to be about, though he did see smoke coming out of a number of stovepipes. He was about to step back when hoof sound hit him with its tap-tap of warning, not loud but plain, certainly moving this way. At about the same time he heard the skreak of greaseless buggy wheels.

That last would be Pike with Bunny and Bender. But who were the horsebackers? Helpers or enemies? Didn't hardly seem time enough for Luce to be coming along with that banker. What if this were a couple of Gourd and Vine gunhawks!

Rafe figured he'd better find out.

He slipped the spur off his heel, left Bathsheba on grounded reins. Hard to tell, the way sound slapped around, which was hoofs and which was echoes, but, it looked a poor bet to wait till they got here.

Scurrying along the bank's back wall, he reached the alley formed by the flank of the Big Bun Bakery, the smells coming out of this near overwhelming him. His stomach went into a spasm of protest as Rafe, hard-faced, plunged into the passage, catfooting streetward through a clutter of tumbleweeds, cans, broken glass and wind-whipped, twisted tore-apart papers. He stopped, gun in hand, when he was close to the street, all his faculties screwed wire tight, edgily listening a spell before popping his head out.

He needn't have got such a sweat up. It was Luce and Alph Chilton making the hoof sound. They were just coming past the front of the Cow Palace, the banker scowling and wagging his lip like a sore-backed bull with a mouthful of larkspur. Rafe, making ready to fade back through the rubbish, went suddenly stiff as his glance crossed a face in the harness shop doorway.

The light wasn't good, the range a full eighty strides across hoof-pocked dust with the guy pulling back into deeper shadow, but Rafe would of swore it was the feller he'd left tied up in the woods the last time he'd gone to the bank to see Chilton—one of the pair Spangler'd staked out at Pike's! If the guy hadn't ducked Rafe might never have seen him.

He went cold all over. Were the rest of them here, stashed around between buildings, or was this ranny on his own, left in town to keep cases? Either way he spelled trouble.

Rafe softly cursed. He was sure enough wedged between a rock and a hard place. He couldn't leave the guy loose to go running to Spangler.

Keeping narrowed stare bitterly pinned to the doorway, Rafe scanned his chances. Last thing he wanted was to rouse the town, and any sudden commotion, or gunplay, could do it. It wasn't likely whoever ran the shop had opened yet; so if he started across the road, both of them knowing he had the guy cornered, the feller was pretty near bound to shoot.

The wheel skreaks had quit. Though he couldn't see it without poking his neck out again, Pike must have the buggy in front of the bank. And the horsebackers had apparently arrived there, too. 'Couldn't this have waited till the bank opened for business?' he heard Chilton say in a voice gruff with outrage. Saddle leather popped and boots thumped ground, and Bunny was tartly saying through the protest of buggy springs, 'Stand around in plain sight with his arms full of money?'

'I haven't seen any money yet!'

'You'll see it,' Pike said, 'when you get that door open—'

'What're *you* doing here?'

'Somebody has to be a witness to this.'

Muttering something about 'highly irregular' Chilton was unlocking the bank's front door when Rafe staring hard, suddenly made up his mind. A man could swing just as high for a sheep as a goat in this country and, since he dared not leave that feller loose, he yelled with his gun up, 'Come outa that doorhole. *Andale! Pronto!*'

Brick chips stung the side of his face. Muzzle-flame bloomed in the harness shop shadows. Firing at the flash Rafe saw Spangler's man stumble out of the doorway clutching his side, lurch two crazy steps in a kind of half circle and crumple into the dust.

Shouts and the slapping of thrown-up windows came through the stomping clatter of echoes as Rafe, diving into the street, gun lifting, ran toward the huddle of statue-like shapes before the bank's open door, the gallop of horses hammering hard at his heels.

Only thing that surprised him was that nobody fired. In all that confusion of cries and called questions it was hard to hold firm to any kind of a course. He saw Chilton in the entry, white-faced, eyes about to roll off his cheekbones. He shoved his free hand against Pike's shoulder. 'Inside! Inside!' He tried to will them to move.

Some excited fool yelled, *'They're stickin' up the bank!'* and Rafe, twisting around, saw Brownwater Bill and a flustered looking badge-packer piling off their ears-back, eye-rolling horses in a fog of lemon dust. He saw more dust, far out, a long balloon-edged boiling line of it.

He stood with sinking heart, all his hopes and defenses toppling. Then he grabbed a fresh breath. 'Get 'em inside, Sheriff, an' hurry it up!' He ran to Bill's rearing horse and snatched free the rifle, levering a cartridge into the chamber. Some of the men hurrying out of near houses sprinted for cover as Rafe put a blue whistler over their heads. He loosed a couple of more to make sure they kept going, and ducked into the bank in the wake of the others, slamming the door.

The rest of this tune he was going to have to play by ear, but he could still take some of the heat off his Pa; and he was glad, looking around, to see that someone had thought to stuff a tow sack for him which the old man was clutching against his chest like it was heavy. And he noticed how Chilton's piggish eyes, though darting around, kept sneaking back to it.

Now, pushing forward, Rafe said, 'Let's get this over with.' His stare speared the banker. Sheriff Ed said, getting his wind up.

'What're we here for? What's goin' on?'

'We're here,' Rafe said, 'to get shed of that mortgage Chilton holds against Gourd and Vine. Anything in them papers, banker, says we can't clear the whole debt off right now?'

Chilton hemmed and hawed, plainly dissatisfied. He looked uneasy, almost frightened, Rafe thought, but the glances he kept stabbing about didn't seem to pick up much in the way of encouragement. He finally said, 'No-o,' in a tone so reluctant it made Brownwater snort. Rafe said, 'All right. Dig 'em up. And, while you're at it, fetch out your receipt book. Meanwhile,' he sniffed, 'let's have some paper an' one of them steel pens. Bender's goin' to scratch his John Henry to a piece of writin' Pike's here to put in the right lingo an' notarize.'

Pike's brows shot up, but he didn't say anything. He pulled up the swivel, seating himself at Chilton's fine desk and squaring the paper the banker got for him. He picked up the pen, examining it critically. Then he uncorked the ink and looked up at Rafe. 'What's it to be?'

'A will,' Rafe grinned. 'The last will and testament of Jeremiah Bender. You can put that down with the appropriate flourishes.' He handed the rifle to Ed Sparks, Chilton's tin-badge. 'Sheriff, you better stand over by the door where the riffraff can get a look at you. Interruptions at a time like this could be downright painful to some of those concerned.' Tapping his six-shooter he looked significantly at Chilton; and the banker, noticeably blanching, made haste to reveal a kind of parched approval.

'Now,' Rafe said, waving Chilton away, 'are you ready, Mr. Notary, to record the bequeaths an' stipulations?'

'Quite ready,' Pike nodded, peering ferociously at his pen.

Rafe, glancing around as though to make sure all were listening, said, 'Everything belonging to J. Bender when he dies, including all lands, chattels, equipment, cash, and all notes payable of whatsoever nature, shall be divided equally, between his daughter Luce and his son Duke.'

In the startled quiet Pike, looking up, seemed about to say something when, for the first time since they'd reached town, the old man spoke. 'This is truly Rafe—my first born,' he said in a trembling, anguish-roughened voice, stretching out a groping hand which Luce, pushing nearer, hastily prisoned in her own. The old man hardly noticed, his pale, blind stare shiningly fixed on things that were not in this place. 'He was always that way, always thinking of others. But I can't let this stand—it's not right. Luce and Duke, they've been with me, had my love, sharing for all these years my days and substance—'

'Nevertheless,' Rafe growled, red-faced, 'they'll have this too. All of you, hear me! I'll have no part of it!'

'My son. My son—'

'We'll get to me,' Rafe said, breaking in again. 'You got that, notary? Got it all down?'

'All down,' Pike said, 'hard and fast. Everything to Luce and Duke.'

'Now write this,' Rafe said, meeting Brownwater's stare. 'Includin' all stones and minerals that may be found on the land, *providing* that one Rafe Bender, acknowledged first son of Jeremiah Bender, and so described in the hearing of these witnesses, be installed and maintained as administrator of this estate and subsequently employed as manager of all above-named lands, chattels, equipment, cash, minerals and so forth for a period of five years and beginning on this date. You got all that?'

'Got it,' Pike said, looking up with a smile. 'But what if they don't agree?'

'If they don't agree, or attempt to have this will set aside, the whole estate, and every last part of it, reverts to the Territory of Arizona.'

'Mr. Bender,' Pike said, 'is this your wish?'

The old man's sightless eyes were fixed unblinkingly on Rafe. 'Yes,' he said. 'I'll put my name to it.'

Pike, with the pen, made a few more scratches.

'Before you fix a place for the names,' Rafe said, leaning over the surgeon's shoulder, 'there's one more line you better git in. Case of Pa's death by violence, or any reason other than natural causes, the whole shebang goes back to the Territory.'

From the door Sparks said, where he stood with Brownwater's rifle, 'Bunch of hairpins boilin' into—'

'The Bender crew!' Luce cried, white as egg shells.

Rafe, seeming hardly to notice her words, jerked the kind of a nod you might look to get from one who had just busted loose of his picket pin. 'Ready for the signin'?' he grunted at Pike.

'Just about,' Bunny's dad said. 'Mr. Bender, you're first.'

Luce helped him over. 'I'm afraid,' Bender sighed, 'I never learnt how,' and Rafe, watching the banker, saw the shock in Chilton's stare.

'Just make your mark,' Pike said. 'Everyone in this room will be witness. Here, let Bunny hold that sack for you.'

Luce put the pen in the old man's fingers, guiding the gnarled and trembling hand. One by one the others stepped up and signed. Rafe, coming back from the door, said then, 'Now we'll take care of that note, Mr. Chilton.'

The banker's eyes juned around like a

boxful of crickets. He stood there like he had stepped in hot glue.

'Well?' Rafe said, and it got powerfully quiet.

If ever a man looked caught out it was Chilton. He dug at his collar, 'I—I can't seem to find them.'

'What can't you find?'

The banker flapped his hands helplessly. 'The papers—I seem to've mislaid them.' The man squirmed in his clothes, peered distractedly at his sheriff. Bunny, with Bender's sack under one arm and the other hand carelessly holding a pistol, was likewise giving Sparks a close regard. Sweat came out on his cheeks like dew. But nothing else came out of him.

Chilton squirmed some more and finally said, 'I suppose it really doesn't matter so long's I give him a receipt and mark it paid in the ledger?'

'Might not matter to you,' Rafe said, 'but we're campin' right here till them notes is turned over.'

Chilton's face got red. 'I've told you I can't find them—'

'You want us to think somebody stole 'em?'

'I don't care what you think,' the banker snarled. 'It is certainly not my habit to mislay important papers! I'll give him a receipt marked "paid in full" and the deed—'

'I reckon that'll be bindin' enough, long as we've got this flock of witnesses.'

Brownwater took the tow sack from Bunny and dropped it on the desk. The dull clink of metal was plainly audible. Audible too was the sound of hoof beats, and still Chilton stood there. 'Spangler,' Rafe said, 'won't be no help to you.'

The banker looked pretty wild, but he got pen and paper. The faint babel of outside voices swelled as the pen scratched into its final flourish. Chilton, sanding it, got up, dug into his safe, and, still clutching the paper, turned around with the deed. Rafe put a hand out.

'I'll count this first,' Chilton growled, pulling the string off the neck of the tow sack. He opened it up, took one look and went rigid.

'Think careful,' Rafe grinned, 'before you lay down your character.'

'I'm not trading that mortgage,' the banker yelled, livid, 'for no bag of iron washers!'

Rafe looked at him coldly. 'You'll trade,' he said, 'or produce that note. You ain't dealin' with no ol' man now. Any damn fool can slap a X on a paper! What these folks'll be plumb anxious to see is how a gent smart as you can make thirty thousan' outa the five Pa borried.'

'Sparks!' Chilton shouted, beside himself.

'Arrest this man! At once—*do you hear?*' So wild did he look he seemed almost to be frothing.

The sheriff, peering over the bore of Bill's rifle, said, 'The worm has turned,' and showed a slow grin. 'What'd you do, forge the old man's name or change the amount?'

Whatever he had done, it was a cinch the banker had not expected to be faced with it. He looked to be standing on the brink of apoplexy. His mouth was working but no words came. There was a twitch in his cheek and the papers skidded out of his shaking hand. Brownwater, retrieving them, laid them in front of the dispassionate Pike who, considering them briefly, affixed his seal. Brownwater wheezed the papers over to Bender. 'There you are, sir. Lock, stock an' barrel.'

Chilton, glassy-eyed, sagged into a chair.

It was then that the silence outside became noticeable.

Spangler's harsh voice called, 'Sheriff, can you hear me?'

'Speak on,' Sparks said.

'I guess you know what we want. You sendin' him out or do we come in after him?'

'If you're yapping about Chilton—'

'I'm talkin' about that bank-robbin' Rebel what calls hisself "Rafe"! We've got the place plumb surrounded! You givin' 'im up or ain't you?'

'He hasn't robbed any bank,' Sparks told them mildly.

'Don't give me that! The whole town seen—'

'Spangler,' Rafe called, 'is Duke Bender out there?'

'An' if he is?'

'You better tell him his father, in front of six witnesses, just made a will—his last will an' testament. Maybe we ought to have Pike read it to him.'

'You ain't pullin' no wool over *my* eyes!'

'Not fixin' to. Just tryin' to keep Duke from cuttin' himself out of what he's got comin'—'

'I'll look out fer Duke's interests!'

'Then you better help him listen.' Rafe, scowling, said, 'If you got the bank surrounded, another two-three minutes ain't goin' to make no never-mind, is it?'

A suspicious silence hung over the street. Then those in the bank heard the muttered sounds of a fierce altercation, after which Duke's prissy tones said, sneering, 'Go ahead. Let him read it.'

Pike, picking up a copy of the will, waddled over to the door, Sparks stepping aside for him. Rafe, while the surgeon-turned-notary was plowing through the whereases and aforesaids, slipped out the side door. The pair of rifle-packing punchers Spangler'd set to watch this exit had, the better to hear, drifted back to the bank's front corner, were now standing hipshot, faces half turned toward the notary's voice. Bathsheba, Rafe remembered, had been left behind the building.

A call would fetch her, ground-tied or not. It would also spin those rifles into focus. Rafe wasn't anxious to shoot those two fellers, and it wasn't very likely he could slip up behind them. He could probably a sight easier get to the mare.

The will would stop Duke, but it wouldn't stop Spangler. Someway Rafe had to get the drop on him; the crew would take Spangler's orders. Rafe doubted they would pay any attention to Duke. What was needed here, if a man wasn't craving to wade through blood, was another diversion. The terms of the will wouldn't be shock enough to keep Spangler's grip long away from his shooter.

Rafe skinned back to the mare, hardly believing even when he was slipping off her headstall he had actually reached her without triggering an alarm. He batted her nose away from his face, tossed reins and bridle against the wall of the bank. He had a terrible hankering to jump on her back when he thought of the odds he was fixing to buck. But he turned her around, hearing the drone of Pike's words, aimed her straight at the woods and, with a wild coyote yell, cuffed her hard with his hat.

Not waiting to watch, he ran on around the far side of the bank, coming into the street just as three of the crew, with shouted orders from Spangler, kicked their horses into a run. Though the unexpected sight of him obviously startled them, not one of them attempted to pull up or swerve. Reaching for their weapons they came, three abreast, straight at him.

Rafe jerked his pistol, firing as soon as it cleared the hoslter. The middle horse reared and, toppling sideways, crashed into the one on its left, kicking frantically. Something jerked at Rafe's vest. The *pfutt pfutt* of slugs was around him like hornets. He shot the third horsebacker out of his saddle and ran on, trying in the confusion of kaleidoscoping shapes to sight Spangler. The shouts and gunblasts beat at him like hammers. A whickering riderless horse slamming past nearly bowled him over and then, unbelievably, the street was empty, the drumming of hoofbeats rapidly fading in the south.

In front of the Cow Palace a man at the edge of its porch staggered upright. Another one's head came up back of a horse trough. Motionless, legs tangled, lay the horse Rafe had shot. There were three more still shapes between the bank and the harness shop.

Sparks, talking over the barrel of his rifle from one of the knocked-out windows behind Rafe, said, 'All right, boys. Any pistol-bangin' jasper wantin' a fair shake from me had better tromp into sight with both paws up an' empty.'

The feller back of the horse trough let go of his hog-leg and, raising his dew-claws, got to his feet. The gent by the edge of the Cow Palace porch didn't appear to be heeled and had already stuck up his hands. Rafe, gun in fist and still cruising the street, didn't pay Sheriff Ed no more mind than a gopher. All his bitter attention when he slogged to a stop seemed glued to the third downed shape so shrunkenly huddled in its bottle-green coat with an arm twisted under it, the yellow curls fluttering in the dust of the street. It was Duke and he was dead. And the pair with their hands up cringed away from Rafe's stare.

Rafe looked back into that dead face and thought of all the times he had covered for the boy, all the scrapes he'd pulled Duke out of, all the risks so recently grappled—wasted, gone like a gutted candle.

Firm steps drew near, an arm came out, a hand clamped warm and hard on Rafe's shoulder. 'You've nothing to reproach yourself with,' Pike wheezed. 'You done more than most would—'

Rafe shook off Pike's arm. 'Who killed him?'

Sparks said, coming, 'That damned

crooked Spangler. We're well rid of both of them; and you sure cut the ground out from under Alph Chilton. He's still in there lookin' like the sky fell on him. Mebbe we can have a little peace around here now.' His glance cut from Rafe to Pike and back. 'Wouldn't consider a job as my deppity, would you?'

Rafe pushed past him, walking away from them. Sparks, looking after him, shook his head. 'Still thinkin' about that worthless brother.' He fetched his scowl to the pair with their hands up. 'All right, you two, find your horses an' drift. I don't want to see your ugly mugs again.'

* * *

But Sparks was wrong about Rafe. His mind was on Spangler. Even hollowed out like he was and half groggy, the range boss' killing of Duke made a kind of queer sense.

The guy had had to hit something, and to him it must have seemed Duke had been party to the terms of Bender's will. The thing that kept banging around in Rafe's head was Spangler clearing out like that while the man responsible for most of his hard luck was still above ground. It wasn't natural.

He said as much when Bunny, a little breathless, caught up with him.

She looked at him big-eyed. 'But he did—I

saw him! Right after he shot Duke and Sheriff Ed knocked that second fellow, Kramer, out of the saddle. Spangler flung himself flat on his horse and dug steel; it was him quitting that way that took the heart out of the rest of them. He's gone, all right. He's probably halfway to Carlsbad.'

'I dunno,' Rafe said, continuing to scowl while his scrinched-up stare smoldered into the southern distance.

'Is killing all you can think of?' Bunny cried. She jerked her hand from his arm with a withering look. 'Go on! Take after him! I don't know why I should be worrying about you!' Wheeling away she went off, stiff-backed, to join her father who stood talking by the Mercantile with Bender and the sheriff.

Rafe guessed with a shrug she likely had the truth of it. Spangler, whatever else, was certainly no fool. He would have seen the cards weren't coming his way with Duke's big brother sitting tall in the leather. He probably figured what he had from stealing Gourd and Vine horses was at any rate better than a hole in the head.

Peering around for Brownwater, Rafe appeared pretty disgusted when he spotted Bill and Luce with their heads bent together. Godfrey Moses! More of that love gush!

But when Luce stepped back, straightening, he could see she had the rock in her fist, the one he'd tossed Bill in the woods this morning while they'd waited for Bunny to fetch her pa to the bank. Luce, he thought, looked pretty excited as, arm linked in Bill's, they struck off for the augmented group around Bender. Most folks, Rafe reminded himself sourly, rather tended to get their wind up when gold came into the conversation.

He reckoned he might as well go hunt Bathsheba and head for the ranch.

* * *

The low-hanging clouds bulged fatly, dark with rain. The dank pungent smell of it grayly clung to the town's grimy buildings, the warped false fronts, the spur-scarred planks and hoof-tracked dust of the windless street.

Too tired really to sort out his thoughts, Rafe decided this weather was enough to depress anyone, and let it go at that. He whistled two or three times the signal he'd taught the skewbald to answer and, when this failed to fetch her, set off for the bosque. She'd either gone too far to hear, seemed like, or was too busy foraging to pay him any mind.

He couldn't remember when he'd been so whipped out. This clammy air stuck the shirt to his shoulders and brewed a discomfort where the belts crossed his belly, and the dreary look of that droopy woods pressed down like the lid of a coffin.

God, he was cheerful!

Luce, he reckoned, would probably marry that puncher. With what she'd come into when the Old Man kicked off they'd be pretty well fixed—a heap better than most in these parlous times. Not that he envied them! He'd traveled too long by himself, been too free, to look with much favor on being pinned down with the problems of a ranch—not to mention the gold or the burdens—he grimaced—of double harness! Nope, he sure wasn't cut out for that.

He rasped stubbly cheek, thought of Bunny, and scowled.

The brush of the bosque and the half-stripped trees, conjuring as these did the other times he'd been in them, were harder on his mood than that depressing damn street. The leaves hung as limp as a parson's coat tails. He had no idea where to look for the mare. He whistled again, shoving on through the brush, half-minded to settle for a bed at the hotel. Then he heard a faint whicker and pulled up to let her find him.

After three or four minutes he remembered what he was standing there for and whistled again. When she still didn't come he started testily after her; sometimes she could be about as obstinate as a mule.

The spindling trees grew thicker in here. He was beginning to work up a sweat with all this bumbling around. Once more he whistled and heard her answer off to the left. Pushing through a scratchy thicket he broke into a forty-foot clearing and saw her, tied with a cotton rope around her neck.

While he was staring a gun went off. The clearing spun dizzily. Rafe didn't hardly know he was hit till he found himself peering up off the ground into the blurred grinning face of Jess Spangler. He saw the gun tip again and frantically rolled. Spangler fired twice before Rafe got his own pistol out of its holster. Desperately Rafe raised it, feeling the bite of fresh pain along his ribs, hearing screams somewhere back of him and suddenly remembering he'd forgotten to reload. Spangler crazily was running toward him when Rafe squeezed the trigger. Six feet away he saw Spangler crumple; and then Bunny Pike had him tight in her arms and he knew everything was going to be all right.